# BELLS ACROSS THE ICE

BY

*JESSE COLT*

To: Victoria's Flowers
Seasons Greetings
Thanks for the excellent service!
Jesse Colt

© Copyright 2004 Jesse Colt. All rights reserved.

No part of this publication may be reproduced, stored in a retrieval system, or transmitted, in any form or by any means, electronic, mechanical, photocopying, recording, or otherwise, without the written prior permission of the author.

Printed in Victoria, Canada

**Note for Librarians:** a cataloguing record for this book that includes Dewey Classification and US Library of Congress numbers is available from the National Library of Canada. The complete cataloguing record can be obtained from the National Library's online database at: www.nlc-bnc.ca/amicus/index-e.html

ISBN 1-4120-0871-9

# TRAFFORD

**This book was published *on-demand* in cooperation with Trafford Publishing.** On-demand publishing is a unique process and service of making a book available for retail sale to the public taking advantage of on-demand manufacturing and Internet marketing. **On-demand publishing** includes promotions, retail sales, manufacturing, order fulfilment, accounting and collecting royalties on behalf of the author.

Suite 6E, 2333 Government St., Victoria, B.C. V8T 4P4, CANADA
Phone       250-383-6864         Toll-free     1-888-232-4444 (Canada & US)
Fax           250-383-6804         E-mail        sales@trafford.com
Web site    www.trafford.com    TRAFFORD PUBLISHING IS A DIVISION OF TRAFFORD HOLDINGS LTD.
Trafford Catalogue #03-1239      www.trafford.com/robots/03-1239.html

10     9     8     7     6     5     4     3

# BELLS ACROSS THE ICE

by

JESSE COLT

**Dedication**

**This book is dedicated to Mary Simpson who co-wrote this novel. Mary loves all animals and mankind in general.**

**RE: Christine Dix (cover artist)**

Christine Dix is emerging as one of Canada's premiere Equine and Western artists. Christine studied art at the University of Calgary and Alberta College of Art and Design. Her work has been displayed at many of the major art galleries in Calgary and Western Canada. Her accomplishments include innumerable ribbons and awards at various art shows. For several years she has been selected as the cover and poster artist for Alberta Standardbred Horse Association Yearling Sale. Her work has been juried into the prestigious Calgary Exhibition and Stampede Art Auction.

Christine is an art instructor and a judge of children's art at local fairs. She has done numerous commission works for equine owners in Western Canada. Christine lives in Black Diamond, Alberta, where she works full time as an artist and painter.

*Bells Across the Ice*

**RE: Jesse Colt (author)**

Jesse was raised in Foxwarren Manitoba, Canada's tiny hockey capital. His education includes an Engineering Degree from the University of Manitoba and Business Administration from McMaster University. Jesse has practiced Engineering in most Canadian provinces and territories. He is currently the Engineering Manager for Prairie West Technical Services.

Jesse ranches in the Alberta foothills near Bragg Creek. He is an award winning Cowboy Poet and his novels have been short listed in the Eppies. He has several books published and more due for publication in the near future.

He is a registered Professional Engineer and a member of the Academy of Western Artists and the Alberta Cowboy Poetry Association. Jesse has been invited to perform his Cowboy Poetry in venues ranging from the local bars along the dusty Cowboy Trail to the glitz of Las Vegas.

*Bells Across the Ice*

# CHAPTER ONE

Far to the north, farther even than the frozen expanse of Great Bear Lake and north of where the last thin stands of timber yielded to the tundra, endless gloom had taken command of the ice packs. The heavy veil of the arctic night cloaked a barren landscape and allied with billowing dark clouds to choke away the last faint light from the desolate scenery below.

Lost on this dreary carpet, three tiny luminescent domes clustered together like faint white mushrooms crouching in the darkness. The silent cones were illuminated by the glow of sputtering oil lamps radiating through the translucent walls of the igloos. These sturdy snow bulwarks sheltered a small band of nomadic hunters. The bold searchers had ventured into this desolate region and would turn their eager huskies south as soon as the night sky cleared and allowed the bright stars to guide them back across the wasted landscape.

Still farther north, almost to the very limit of the compass, the scene remained timeless and unchanging beneath a cloudless sky. Rough ice ridges heaved their ragged shoulders up from the black pack ice. Irregular drifts of snow broke the faint horizon and cringed under the harsh blasts sweeping down from the north. Here, the restive snow flowed across the endless white tundra, driven forward on the stinging breath of the polar wind. The frozen crystals drifted a scant meter over the familiar surface, an endless white river undulating across the featureless terrain.

These were not the soft plump flakes of the southern regions. The perpetual stream was formed of ice particles that had swirled around the tip of the North Pole, tasted the frigid air of the Russian arctic and endured the solitude of the endless Siberian night. The numbing arctic gusts granted the crystals an eternal life, shifting them restlessly over the polar ice caps like lost souls condemned to eternal wandering across the wasted landscape.

The ghostly tide surged on polar ice, now polished to a glistening hue by the endless passage of the uneasy stream. The frozen crystals gathered speed, skating over the burnished surface, tinkling like tiny bells heralding the coming of another Christmas season.

Without warning, they shattered against a barrier of ragged steel and corrugated aluminum forms. The frozen steel bordered a sprawling communication centre buried in the timeless snow. High over the cheerless scene, a stunted Christmas tree jutted up from the frozen peak of the largest warehouse.

The tormented pine stretched its sparse limbs skyward, flaunting coloured lights to the prim communication towers trembling in the gale that surged though the taunt guy-wires. The multicolored lights and spindly tree were recent arrivals to this outpost, carried in on a thundering Hercules. This mammoth aircraft regularly broke the spell of the hushed night, expelling the necessities of life into this remote installation before dashing southward to the familiar comfort of its warm hangers and attentive crews.

Deep inside one of the frozen metal huts, Jim Thorndyke shrugged his lean shoulders into yet another heavy sweater. He did not bother to peer out the frost-encrusted window of his tiny room, for the scenery never changed. The endless panorama merely contracted or expanded, depending upon the whim of winds that stirred the passive snow or ushered in southbound blizzards that toyed with the faint horizon.

The sparsely furnished room was still cold. Despite Jim's efforts to seal the cracks around the frosted window and the addition of two electric heaters, the cutting wind forced its icy tentacles past the insulation, clutching at his chilled bones. Jim seldom ventured from his artificial womb during the long winter months. His comrades hiked, snow-shoed and ran skidoos, but he was content to remain in his self-imposed exile. The long arctic winter held no charms for Jim Thorndyke.

He located his bulky mitts and then wrestled the down parka from its cramped closet. Struggling into the huge windbreaker, he glanced at his watch and frowned at the pallid artificial tree cowering in a corner of his cubicle. The miniature lights were winking bravely against the chill of the room, making a desperate attempt to bring the spirit of Christmas to a soul that had long forgotten the true meaning of the season.

Jim knew Nester would soon be at his door, pounding and shouting for him to hurry and showering him with curses in coarse Ukrainian. He glanced at his suitcase, half-packed and waiting expectantly beside the freakish little tree. The luggage was crowded against the few presents he was carrying south.

His Christmas list grew shorter each year. Since the divorce, there were fewer friends to buy for and almost no cards to anticipate. The girls, at least the daughter who was still communicating with him, seemed satisfied with a Christmas cheque. Cheques simplified the shopping. He scowled at the exorbitant jeweled watch for his girlfriend, still unwrapped, an awkward task he would avoid until he was back in Calgary.

Ingried hardly qualified as his girlfriend. She only pretended to be when he came south for a few days and needed the companionship of her warm available body. He knew that by the time he had packed his heavy bags and trudged up the steel steps of the gloomy north bound Hercules again, Ingried was no longer his. She was available for any high roller with the money to show her a good time.

It didn't bother Jim, not like it should have and he felt no sense of guilt that he was leaving her behind and flying to the Caribbean with Nester. He had ordered the expensive watch on impulse. He knew the jewel-encrusted timepiece was no more reliable than a cheap one, but the gold and diamonds would please her 14-karat mind. The elegant doll resting beside the watch was for her pampered child. What had possessed him when he ordered her daughter this extravagant gift? Ingried's brattish offspring and Jim had developed a passionate dislike for one and other. Buying her daughter's present was just some left over reaction from Christmases' long past when he had bought gifts for children less demanding and arbitrary than her spoiled brat.

He examined the small calendar tacked to the bleak wall. The days were marked over in heavy black and red ink, marking his shifts on and days off. Today was December 17. *Damn it*! Tania's letter had still not arrived!

The eagerly awaited letter was already late, but this was typical of Tania, his younger daughter, perhaps the world's worst procrastinator. He remembered the emotional phone calls they had shared just after the divorce, but once he had started this assignment in the Arctic the calls had become difficult to arrange. Now it seemed she was never in when he phoned.

Predictably, her letter arrived each year just before Christmas, like some precious lifeline to his past. Her annual message was always lengthy, a delight to read. The sparkling lines told of her hopes and dreams, her trials and triumphs throughout the year. Infinitely more important to Jim were her expressions of eternal faith in her father, a belief he often found waning in himself.

Tania was in college now, studying journalism. With a little hard work and her personal dreams answered, someday she would become a writer. Her annual letters were long enough to occupy him for hours, even days, reading and rereading the glowing lines. Now, instead of her familiar sprawling handwriting, the words came on crisply typed sheets, probably created on the expensive computer and printer he had given her for her last birthday.

He longed desperately for the letter! Without this precious gift, Christmas would be devoid of its last star. The season would become as forlorn as a discarded Christmas tree, shedding its brown needles in the warmth of March with only a few pieces of ripped tinsel to remind the world of its former splendor.

He thought of Christine, his older daughter. This memory was a painful one. She had not spoken to him since the divorce. The cheques that reached her were still cashed, but the letters went unanswered. He knew that Anne, his wife, could always give him Christine's new address, but he wasn't speaking to Anne either. Not since her lawyer had threatened him with legal action if he didn't hurry the alimony through.

Christine's face flashed before his eyes again, full of anger and hurt. He wondered if there was any pain deeper than that of a lost daughter. Was there anything he could do to bridge the dreadful gap?

His dismal thoughts were interrupted by an impatient pounding on his fragile door. He flung it open, trying to dismiss the memory. He snapped off the light switch, plunging the room and the freakish little tree into darkness.

"Hey! Jim, you look like you seen a fucking ghost. What's the matter? You been sipping your Christmas presents early?" Nester chuckled.

Jim stepped into the cold hallway and scowled down at his compact companion. Nester was a short wiry Ukrainian, possessed of a great physical strength far out of proportion to his medium frame. His untrimmed hair and full beard were sprinkled with gray in contrast to his ruddy complexion. Nester had the cold agate eyes of a killer, flinty as the northern ice. He required less sleep and more alcohol than anyone Jim had ever known. He could go for days without a good night's rest and still spend the evenings matching drinks with men twice his size. Everyone in the Company seemed to know Nester. Each time there was a major project requiring the crews be driven a bit harder or a job completed ahead of schedule, they called on Nester. He was everywhere cajoling, boasting, cursing the lack of progress and demanding every detail be completed to perfection. He drove his crews as he drove his iron body. They gave him more than he had any right to expect and he rewarded them both with cold beer and generous shots of premium Alberta rye.

Jim had known Nester before they had come north, when they had both worked for another organization, back when his former company still had a soul and cared about its people.

Nester seldom talked about his past or his family anymore. Jim knew he had a marriage gone bad like his own and two teenagers living with his wife. Nester had coaxed him north, persuading him to sign on with him one day when Jim was weak and hung over. He had never regretted the decision. The job was distant and remote from his earlier life. The pay was excellent. The hours were long, but it kept his mind off his unhappy past and Nester refused to let him indulge in self-pity. When times got bad, there was always the bottle of smooth Alberta rye!

Nester was the most energetic person Jim had ever met. Despite his lack of formal education there was never a piece of equipment that he couldn't repair and leave in better working order than when it had left the factory.

Jim scrutinized the hard features again. He could never understand what attractions Nester's lean frame or coarse humor held for the opposite sex. But whatever had driven his former wife away, seemed to lure the majority of the female population to his brash character.

"Hey. It's warmer out today. Only minus 36 C this morning. Hardly any wind. Do you want to walk over instead of taking the damned dark tunnel?"

Jim frowned at his companion. Even the steel ringed tunnel was an icebox, unheated and cloaked with dripping frost. It was almost as cold as the surface, but without the driving wind that slashed razor sharp ice crystals against exposed flesh. Nester's parka was unzipped! The huge mittens dangled on tethers at his side.

"Christ, Zary, you're the one full of alcohol! I'll take the tunnel. Thank you."

Nester led him into the dark steel burrow connecting their sleeping quarters with the mess hall. During the night, someone had strung a battered set of Christmas lights up at the entrance. The frozen paint was already flaking off the bulbs and some of the lights had burned out, but still, they added a faint sense of Yuletide to the somber atmosphere of the isolated post.

"Christmas!" Nester snorted. "The bloody airport will be jammed again. I hope we don't have to wait all day in Calgary for a fucking taxi to the hotel," he muttered a short curse in Ukrainian.

He was flying south with Jim to the Caribbean. They would arrive in Calgary on the 23 of December and the next day they would be in the tropics, pouring on sun tan oil and sipping rum laced cocktails. A few years ago it would have seemed sacrilegious to leave the crisp Canadian snow and gaily decorated Christmas trees behind. No more! It was easier in the Caribbean, without the leering ghosts of Christmases' past to haunt them. Jim could have left yesterday, but he had given up his seat, to a friend wanting to visit Winnipeg to be with his family. Now he regretted his act of generosity, for the memories of Christmases past were pressing in again without the southern distractions to keep them at bay.

Jim was eager for a lengthy vacation in a tropical paradise. He would be far from the haunting memories. His only challenge would be his ability to match drinks with the tough, full-bearded Ukrainian in the noisy nightclubs that his brash companion loved to frequent.

They hurried to the mess hall where the welcome smell of strong coffee jolted their senses awake. A gaudy Christmas tree had sprouted in the packed cafeteria. The tables had blossomed red and green decorations in place of their usual austere setting. They pushed into the mess-hall line and Jim watched his companion order a mountain of bacon and eggs. He listened as Nester barked precise instructions to the cooks and heaped the meal unto his plate. Jim collected his own breakfast and followed him to the milk dispenser where Nester added two large glasses to his burgeoning tray.

They joined Bob Risk at one of the tables. Bob was the acting site manager over the holidays, a big gentle man, prematurely bald, with heavy features that broke easily into a pleasant smile. His relaxed manner and genuine concern for his fellow man had made the post a pleasant place to work, under these difficult conditions.

Bob's welcoming smile beamed them over to the table, "Hey, Nester, you know we have to fly those eggs all the way from Ontario. Leave a little for the next shift, eh," he chuckled.

He turned to Jim. "I see you let Rick go out in your place," he smiled his approval across the table and Jim felt a little better. He could last a few more days.

— ♦ —

Jim moved on to the radar tower and the hours crept past. Outside, the distant sun made a faint attempt to color the southern horizon before slipping back into the dark pit that held it captive.

Jim was good at his job and the radar and communication equipment on the site were well maintained. His degree in engineering and the years of practical experience made him ideally suited for this demanding work. He didn't mind the isolation, for the long hours kept him active and left him little time to dwell on his past. He glanced out the window into the arctic night, and then shivered when he thought of Nester.

Nester was overhauling one of the main generators today. The units were barely sheltered from the elements. It would be bitterly cold and the labor could be backbreaking with the limited equipment assigned to this remote site. Still the job would probably be completed in record time and it would give Nester something more to boast and grumble about. The tougher the job, the more he seemed to enjoy it.

Jim finished his reports and tossed the documents into the out basket. The paperwork always took him longer this time of the year. His mind often retreated into the sweet memories and the times when Christmas was filled with the laughter of his daughters and the thrill of the short vacation they shared at New Years. He could find many reasons to blame Anne for their failed marriage much of the year, but at Christmas he was more forgiving.

He pictured Anne again. She really had not been that difficult to live with. He remembered how much she enjoyed Christmas, how hard she had tried to make the last one they shared enjoyable. Their marriage seemed destined to failure, although he often regretted the things he had said to her. His mind was still struggling in the past when Ron Lylyk strolled in and pulled down the hood of his frosted parka. He sauntered to the coffee pot and poured himself a cup of the steaming brew.

"Hey, Jim, you were supposed to go out on the Herc Friday, weren't you?" Ron's quiet voice drawled across the room.

Jim snapped out of his daydream. The word *supposed* had penetrated the thick fuzz blurring his mind. Ron could tell by the startled look on Jim's face that he was expecting a flight out on the southbound Hercules. Jim gaped at Ron, waiting for an explanation.

Ron stirred the coffee, slowly rubbing his chilled fingers. "Yea, some joker in a snow plow rammed into our bird back in Edmonton." he shook his head and laughed. "Took off part of the under-carriage. They say it will be at least a week or ten days before we see another flight in here. Damned shame with Christmas and all. Lots of mail won't make it in till January now."

Jim was on his feet, glowering at Ron. There was no way he was going to spend Christmas here! He wasn't even scheduled to work!

The boredom would drive him nuts!

"Hell!" Jim snapped. "They'll find something else. They can't cancel all the flights. Not just before Christmas!" he tried to hide the emotion in his voice.

"Well, they might find another craft, but remember how long they took the last time one of the regular planes went down. And this year the accountants are struggling to make their numbers for year end. I doubt if we'll see that Herc till the New Year now." He was in no panic. His flight out was not due till mid-January.

Jim knew Ron was right. The big birds were always in demand and their site was well off the main air routes. He frowned at the clock. It was near quitting time. Maybe Nester had better news. He wanted to check the mail again. Perhaps Tania's letter had shown up. Maybe the desperately awaited package had come in on one of the small utility flights or a wayward military aircraft.

— ♦ —

The next days crept past. Each hour brought another happy rumor of a rescheduled Christmas flight, but by the time Jim was sharing his evening drink with Nester, the stories had proved as empty as the windswept landscape stretching from the windows of his small cell. The Herc would be repaired, but skeleton crews, bad weather and lost parts had grounded the versatile machine until after Christmas. He and Nester would miss their holiday flight! The images of the Caribbean sun were swept away in the harsh arctic wind.

Jim cursed his misfortune. It was not the postponed vacation that he regretted. It was the realization that he might have to face the Christmas season and all its familiar ghosts. There would be no diversions to take his mind off his failures except the glasses of premium Alberta rye. He scowled at the bottles lining his desk, the ones he laughingly exchanged with friends on the site every holiday season. They were all that stood between him and the taunting memories of long forgotten Christmases.

Tania's letter had not come! He wondered if the dreaded day had arrived… the time when she no longer cared enough to compose her marvelous annual communication to him. How could he hold out against the mountain of harsh memories that seemed to weigh heavier with each season? Her glowing message was his last hope.

He puffed through the weights in the exercise room, rattling the cold metal with a vengeance and cursing the hard fate that threatened to confine him to this ice-bound steel island. He showered and returned to his room. His shivering hands were pouring his first drink when Nester came pounding on his door. The frosted beard could not hide the flush of excitement that had crept over his lean features.

"Hey! I found us a flight out of here. Are you still packed?" He stood smiling in the doorway waiting for Jim's reaction.

"Zary, you're joking! You must be! There ain't no way out of this Hell-hole. Everyone has been trying for days. What are you talking about?"

Jim could not believe the intense Ukrainian had found an escape route. Still, he allowed himself a small measure of optimism, for Nester seemed to have connections throughout the north and sometimes it seemed everyone owed him a favor.

"Where are your tickets?" Nester demanded. "I can get us into Yellowknife by the 22$^{nd}$ and Risk will pay our airfare to Calgary. I can fax Betty and she will arrange everything. Are you coming?"

Jim was trembling with excitement. Nester had found an escape from the brutal ghosts lurking in the shadows of the Christmas lights. He wanted to shake Nester's hand. If anyone could arrange a flight out it would be Nester.

"Nester! Nester! Tell me you're not lying to me. I can pack in two minutes. Is the transport from Bakers Island coming through?"

"No, it ain't coming. Even better than that! We got our own private plane!" He spotted Jim's glass of rye. "Hey, I need a drink to celebrate. Where you hiding your glasses?"

Jim frowned at the eager figure eyeing the bottle of rye. He began to wonder if Nester was imagining the private plane. There were no charters in this frozen wasteland. He reached for an extra glass on the top shelf of his closet, but he was still watching Nester's face for an answer.

"What are you talking about, Zary? No one charters out of this hole!"

"Sure, one airline. Bear Air. Old Geezer MacCleod still flies out of here."

Jim had never heard of MacLeod or his obscure airline, but then he seldom ventured past the confines of the electrical room.

"Who the hell is Bear Air?" he gasped watching as Nester poured a generous shot of neat rye, tossed back a mouthful and grimaced as the fiery liquid coursed into his cold innards.

"I know Geezer from Winnipeg. He still has a small hanger at the end of our main runway. Been there since before this station was built. He has been around forever and made some flights for the big boys when our own pilots were afraid to get their candy asses off the ground. I've helped overhaul his plane a few times. He's the old Scotsman that flew me and Bruce Biehn out fishing last summer. Geezer has one fare booked to Yellowknife, but he'll chuck him out here and make room for you. He has to drop some generator parts off at a little village called Old Bow. If we help him unload there, he'll take us both to Yellowknife for $500 cash. Hey! It will be a great flight! Better than riding behind the freight in those crowded old Hercs."

Jim wondered who the passenger might be that the air-line could abandon in this isolated post. Who would be willing to pass up an escape from the northern isolation at Christmas? The question was a fleeting one, for he was caught up in the excitement of the moment. He could see himself on the warm beaches and the cold ghosts of Christmases long past were cackling in frustration over his good fortune. Even Tania's missing letter seemed unimportant. He raised his glass to the possibilities.

"Nester, did you clear all this with Risk?"

Nester shrugged. "No problem. He says, go ahead. He has a ton of extra bodies stranded here. We're off tomorrow. I've arranged for Ron to run us out on a snow cat. He tossed back the last of his rye. We leave at nine. I'll see you at breakfast!"

♦ ♦ ♦

## CHAPTER TWO

The harsh clatter of the alarm snapped Jim awake at 6:30 a.m. There was just time for a hearty breakfast and one last chance to wish everyone a Merry Christmas. He had carefully packed the night before, but he had hardly slept from the anticipation of the flight. One last trip to the mail room on the chance that Tania's letter had risen out of the flood of Christmas mail, and then he was out of here.

The trip to the postal station was wasted. The letter had not arrived. Despite this unhappy result, he felt like kid again. His heart was racing like a child who had just been granted a trip to Disneyland. The thought of the pounding surf was already pushing the chill from the frigid room. When Nester and Ron came hammering on his door, he greeted them with an enthusiasm he had not felt in years. They hurried to the cafeteria where the scent of hot coffee mingled with the sharp odor of the fresh pine with its anemic Christmas decorations.

"So you and Zary are flying Bear Air are you?" Risk chuckled. "My, my, my! Well old Geezer has hauled some stranger passengers." He laughed to himself, remembering some story he was not prepared to share with Jim.

"Aw, you should be okay! There aren't that many bars along his flight path." He seemed to be offering Jim some encouragement he did not really feel. "Bear Air, eh?" He laughed again, "all the way south to Yellowknife."

Jim hurried through breakfast and wished his friends the best of the season. He felt a twinge of pity for those who could not share his good fortune, but the euphoria of the moment was still upon him and he would not allow their misfortune to dampen his spirits.

The first light of the false dawn had begun to tinge the distant tundra when they arrived at the rundown hanger. The tiny airdrome was little more than a disintegrating metal shed with the nose of a battered aircraft nudged into the questionable warmth of the snow covered building. Jim eyed the weathered old relic and listened to Ron's slow monotone. Ron knew airplanes and there weren't many that he couldn't describe in detail.

"Gee, Nester. You guys get to fly in a genuine Noorduyn Norseman. Not many people get that opportunity anymore," he chuckled at the prospect.

Nester frowned at Ron. "Hey! I helped him overhaul that engine. This baby will take us anywhere."

"Yea, they were a great little plane in their day," Ron laughed again. "Course this one looks like an old Mark V. Probably built around 1945 or 46. A little bit of aluminum for a frame, but mostly spruce and fabric. This was one of the first planes that had the flaps and ailerons interconnected. It could take off in the length of football field." Jim didn't like the way Ron kept using the past tense.

"I didn't know you were certified to work on aviation equipment, Nester," Ron raised his eyebrows, testing Nester's reaction.

Nester chose to ignore Ron's challenge and booted open the frozen steel door of the hanger.

Jim stood outside for a moment and gaped at the frost-covered relic that was to carry him south. He remembered Risk's laughter. The dilapidated old aircraft was outlined in the pale glow from the hanger. The plane seemed to crouch in the dim light, embarrassed by its rundown appearance. He could see the faded yellow paint under the layers of frost. The color was reminiscent of the World War II aircraft he had seen abandoned at the edges of many airfields in southern Alberta. This craft seemed worn and gaunt. The taut fabric stretched over the fuselage like the giant ribcage of some oversized locust. There were ill-disguised patches where the fuselage had been repaired. These newer scars reflected the faint lights from the hanger like some ancient wounds that had not quite healed over.

Jim examined the taut cable and turn-buckled wires that seemed to be strung everywhere in a valiant effort to hold the stressed airframe together. The frayed aircraft was mounted on shattered skis. The runners did not match. One faded red ski was a recent addition from a salvage yard, the other seemed shorter, a dented silver remnant and part of the original equipment that matched the equally battered airframe. He frowned up at the cabin where one door and two of the small windows had been replaced by weathered plywood sheeting.

He turned to Ron. Their silent companion had not offered him any encouragement regarding the craft's airworthiness. Jim pulled away from the discouraging sight and ducked through the small portal behind Nester's wiry frame.

"Hey! Geezer," Nester shouted. "You got the coffee on yet?"

A stooped figure slowly straightened out of the shadows in the farthest corner of the vacant building, rising up like a frozen mummy stepping from the grave. The vague form tossed the parts he had been cleaning back into an open bucket of gasoline. The acrid fumes from the gaping container stung the frosty air. Greasy hands sought warm mittens while he searched for the sound of Nester's voice in the dim light of a solitary bulb illuminating the cold airdrome. The rigid neck rotated towards the sound of Nester's voice until he spotted his guests struggling to close the protesting door. He moved stiffly across the deck, peering through the gloom like a near-sighted owl trying to identify some faint movement just beyond the range of its vision.

Jim watched him approach. The stumbling figure appeared too old to be flying in the rigors of the arctic. The stooped frame was of average height, but his stature had been worn away by the years. He walked with a slight crouch. His ancient back had grown tired of stretching the cramped muscles in the cold air and had decided not to expend any more energy on such a vain gesture. His face was red and blotchy, the flesh wind burned, slipping down the bone structure like a wax mold that had been left too close to a flame. A week's growth of stained white whiskers contrasted with the ruddy complexion and bulbous scarlet nose. He sniffled loudly and often through dripping nostrils that attracted a regular swipe from his oversized rawhide mittens, a regular motion, like some prehistoric windshield wiper. His eyes were red and watery. He seemed to be having trouble focusing on his guests. He pulled one greasy hand from a stained mitten and extended it to Jim. The grip was warm, almost feverish, but possessed an iron strength that locked on Jim's cold fingers and left him wondering where the ancient frame found such a source of energy.

Nester introduced Geezer and Jim examined the old bush pilot's attire. The oversized parka was grimy and stained with oil. The baggy military trousers were large enough to accommodate several pairs of long underwear, the heavy flannel layers forming an effective shield against the snap of the arctic gusts. In deference to the season, Geezer's drab apparel was complimented by a ridiculous looking Santa Claus hat, complete with a snow white band and tassel. The greasy hands had not yet soiled his Christmas attire and it clung to the thinning hairline in a grim mockery of the season.

Jim stared at the stooped figure and Risk's laughter hung ominously in the chilled air.

"Well, lads, let's hook your snow cat on back and pull her out of the hanger. My Jeep's froze up this morning," Geezer wheezed. His trembling hands fumbled in his pockets for a battered pack of cigarettes. There was a slight Scottish brogue in the gritty voice.

The dour Scotsman directed the maneuver and when the frail craft was facing onto the pack ice, he climbed inside and attempted to fire up the cold engine. The worn pistons sputtered a few times and coughed out ominous puffs of black smoke into the pristine air. The cranky engine refused to run. Jim had gained a better look at the dilapidated airplane squatting on the frozen terrain and decided that he would be just as happy if the old Norseman did not start. He was prepared to wait for the well-maintained and reliable Hercules, even if it meant another ten days on the isolated base.

Nester watched the wheezing pilot's futile efforts for a minute then seized a screwdriver and pried up the cowling. Geezer poked his head out a cracked panel and squinted at Nester. When Nester had tinkered with the oil drenched engine he raised his thumb in signal to Geezer. The craft barked a few times then fired to life, driving another stream of black smoke into the crisp air.

Geezer urged the ragged pistons into a staggering rumble until he judged the engine capable of idling on its own. He led them back inside and huddled near a squat stove, glowing in the center the old building. Despite the roar inside the firebox, the flames were incapable of heating the frost rimmed structure and contented themselves with keeping the large pot of coffee boiling on the glowing surface.

"Well, I'll go shut her down and we can toss the rest of the cargo into the back," Geezer growled.

They hustled through the chill of the night and Jim clambered up the slick aluminum steps and peered inside the darkened bush plane. Several wooden cases were tied to the splintered plywood floor, carelessly secured with rope and strands of rusted wire. Someone had stenciled Old Bow across the battered plywood cases. Jim remembered that their route south would take them through an isolated village somewhere to the northwest of Yellowknife. He squinted into the cockpit. There was one passenger already on board, apparently asleep in the lone passenger seat that had been crammed in behind the pilot and co-pilot's compartments. There was the overpowering smell of liquor in the crisp air. Jim guessed that the huge figure was sleeping off a gigantic hangover in the frosty night.

He examined the sparse accommodations inside the craft. There was only seating for three people. Nester had told him they were dropping a passenger off at their base. Jim wondered again who the unlucky traveler was, for he was sleeping in the precious seat that had been reserved for Jim. Jim was trying to rationalize his dilemma when Geezer began heaving their luggage into the back of his battered craft.

He motioned to the sleeping passenger, "Well, laddies, let's toss that ornery son of a bitch out and we'll be on our merry way!"

Jim clawed his way up the slippery floor and cautiously approached the slumbering occupant. He tapped the gigantic bundled form with his mittened hand, eager to wake him and lay claim to the last southbound seat. The stranger sat motionless, apparently determined to ignore Jim's intrusion. Perhaps the possibility of having to spend Christmas on this isolated base was too much for the silent traveler. Jim jabbed the rigid shoulders, determined to get his attention. The grimy fur trimmed hood glided back off the man's head and Jim recoiled at the sight revealed in the yellow glow of the cabin lights.

The monstrous face was leering directly at him. The evil grin revealed chipped yellow teeth. The heavy head of graying hair was clipped close and fashioned into a rough brush cut. The gaping dark eyes were staring and vacant. His broad face and square chin were covered with gray stubble. It took Jim's numb mind several tortured seconds to comprehend the horror before him. The man was a corpse, frozen into his seat!

Jim leapt away from the hideous specter, tumbling back into the cockpit amid howls of laughter from Nester.

"Jesus Christ! That man is a fucking corpse!" Jim fought to control his breathing.

"Yep, he is a corpse now, ain't he," Geezer sniffed. "You'd be corpse too iffin someone stuck an eight inch blade in your gizzard. The ornery son of a bitch! I'd a stabbed him myself, for sure if I was given half the chance. Guess he finally found an Indian that weren't a-feared of him. Ugly son of a bitch now, ain't he!"

Geezer pushed forward and casually wrapped one arm around the man's shoulder as if he were embracing an intimate friend. He thrust his other bare hand deep into the inside pockets of the dead man's parka and pulled out a set of official looking documents. He waved them proudly at Jim.

"Yep, I hauls them south for the Mounties all the time. They pays me more than five times what I'd get for a normal yappy fare. Course most of them don't favour me with any return business!" he chuckled.

Jim sucked in a slow breath and tried to calm his racing heart. "Jesus Christ" he murmured. "You could have fucking told me!"

Geezer seemed puzzled by Jim's concern. "Yep! You're looking at Weasel Kalhoun. Least what's left of him. Used to be an accountant or a financial manager for some large firm down east. Had one of them worthless jobs a snake wouldn't touch. After he filled his pockets and screwed the company, he came north looking for more easy pickings. Stole what he could and put his blade in anyone who wouldn't play his greedy game. Guess he finally met someone were better with a knife than he were," he mused.

"Well, get him out of there, Laddy. Lesson your fond of sharing you're seat with the likes of him," he chuckled again. "I'll collect him next time I'm back this way. No need to hurry him south. There's one bastard ain't got no loving relatives hoping he'll make it home early for Christmas mass."

Jim searched desperately for Ron and the snow cat. He had had enough! Another few days up here wouldn't kill him. Nester and Geezer could make the trip and take their frozen buddy with them. He wasn't desperate enough to risk his life in a rickety old plane that was little more than a flying hearse.

Jim looked across the shadows to where Ron had parked the agile machine. The snow cat was gone! The receding tracks were already drifting in. He looked into Nester's laughing eyes. He knew the callused Ukrainian was thoroughly enjoying Jim's discomfort.

Jim sucked in a deep breath. He would freeze walking back to camp and there was no sense asking Nester for mercy. The man didn't know the meaning of the word.

"How do we get this bastard out?" Jim stammered.

Nester was at the corpse's feet in a second. "Grab his bloody shoulders and pull him face forward, we can slide the ugly bastard out the back cargo door on his fucking knees," he encouraged.

"Yeah, that's the way to handle him lads. Tilt him forward out the seat and then flip the bastard over. Slide him down the floor on his arse. Them frozen fellows come out real easy once they're out of their seat. I got a bad back, but I'll get the sleigh for his ugly carcass."

They began to wrestle the unyielding corpse. Even in death the massive frame seemed obstinate and uncooperative. The frozen torso was as stiff and inflexible as a rigid side of freezer beef. Kalhoun was hunched forward into a sitting position, determined to cling to his seat. There was just enough room between the oversized seat and the bulkhead to maneuver the massive corpse out. They struggled mightily until the rigid form began to yield. They wrestled the remains part way out of the seat, but the resolute figure seemed to clutch at the narrow aisle, frustrating their efforts.

Jim struggled on the slippery floor, sliding across a patch of slick aluminum sheeting. Nester braced his wiry frame against the frozen bulkhead and put a headlock around the un-yielding neck. The corpse lurched from the seat, just as Jim slipped on the frosty surface. Kalhoun made one last desperate leap forward, pinning Jim between the seat and narrow corridor. Jim felt the bite of pure terror as the corpse began to slide over him. The great whiskered face moved relentlessly downward. The stiff frozen hands stabbed into Jim's stomach as if the corpse still had an evil will of its own. The arctic butcher seemed intent on extracting his vengeance on those who were trying to remove him from the last southbound flight. The corpse was as heavy as a steer. The great immobile form appeared intent on crushing Jim against the frost on the hard aluminum floor. He screamed in terror, trapped beneath the grisly remains between the two front seats. Geezer shuffled back from the hanger in response to the desperate shouts. He poked his head in and squinted through the cabin trying to determine the reason for Jim's pitiful moans.

"Jim, are you okay?" Nester called, certain his friend had suffered some injury from the fall.

"Nester," Jim gasped. "I'm fine; just get that bastard off me! Oh merciful Christ, get him the fuck off me!"

Geezer heaved his stiff shoulders into the aircraft. He pushed in beside Nester where the bearded figure was choking back a fit of laughter. Together they began wrestling the corpse off the moaning figure trapped beneath the frozen hands. At last they succeeded in swinging the unyielding cadaver upright. Jim wriggled free and staggered up on one trembling knee, wiping the sweat off his dripping brow. He caught his breath and found the courage to help drag the rigid remains out of the aircraft and into the cold hanger.

He watched as his callused companions gleefully propped the corpse up in an oily chair and looped a worn extension cord around the rigid torso.

Jim winced at the pathetic figure lashed to the seat. What would happen if someone from the station walked in on the morbid sight? He could imagine Risk collapsing with a massive heart attack.

"Surely you're not going to leave him like this. The man's frozen stiff. Shit, it's Christmas!" Jim protested.

"Hah," Geezer snarled. "Where he's headed for, it won't take them long to thaw him out. Evil son of a bitch. May the fires of Hell be turned up when they see him coming. I'd a stuck the knife in him myself if I'd had half a chance," he repeated. He favored the corpse with a vicious kick to its frozen shins and spat at the icy boots.

Weasel continued his vacant leer at the roof of the old building. His crossed eyes were focused on the layer of frost on the upper beams; oblivious to the insults being heaped on his pathetic remains.

"Well, shit. Reckon you might have a point there!" Geezer grumbled. "Maybe we ought to be more generous with him, seeing as it's Christmas!" He jerked the Santa Claus cap off his own head and jammed it roughly over the thinning hair line of the huge corpse. He snatched a bottle of cheap Scotch from the top of a cluttered shelf. There was still an ounce or two in the grimy bottle. He stared ruefully at the drained bottle. For a moment Jim thought he was going to pour the contents on the corpse, instead he let the remaining booze flow down his throat. He coughed and jammed the bottle into the frozen hands.

"There you are, you ignorant son of a bitch. Now you have a really Merry Christmas!" He wiped his stained mitts against the running nose again.

"Come on; let's get this show on the road, before we freeze the skis into the bloody snow."

Jim turned away from the disgusting spectacle. He could have stood a drink himself.

He followed Geezer's hunched form into the night and watched as the old bush pilot quickly inspected the cargo in the packed freight compartment. Jim scrambled reluctantly into the seat vacated by the cold corpse and examined the interior. The aircraft seemed pieced together with worn scraps of material. Plywood sheets were screwed into the sides of the fuselage and fresh metal studs adorned the hull. The splintered wooden floor was patched with irregular pieces of aluminum sheeting. Wire cables crisscrossed the frame. Jim shuddered at the thought and wondered if it was too late to bolt for the exit.

Geezer pulled a large thermos of hot coffee from his solitary piece of luggage. Jim watched the gnarled hands rummage through a pile of soiled newspapers and garbage at his feet. The trembling fingers extracted three used Tim Horton coffee cups from the pile of rubbish on the floor. The battered wax cups were worn, soiled and stiff from the frost. He pried the frozen lids off. Nester held the containers steady while Geezer's trembling hands splashed the stained receptacles full with steaming coffee.

"Here, we had better pour this before we get airborne. The air can be a little rough this time of year." Geezer forced his stiff neck around and examined the shadowy figure in the back. "Better have a drink, Sonny." He passed the soggy cup to Jim.

"You look a little pale this morning, Sonny! Maybe you're just a nervous flyer!" He winked at Nester and handed Jim a stained cup, full of steaming coffee. A shaky hand pulled his crushed pack of cigarettes from his pocket and Jim winced as the old man struck a match amid the fumes of the cabin.

Jim accepted the weeping cup. He was tempted to throw it out, but the windows were frozen. He watched as Geezer's trembling hands fumbled with the switches and the cockpit assumed an electronic life. The huge mittens hammered the start button. The engine sputtered once then puffed a thick cloud of blue smoke before stalling. Geezer cursed the balky machine, took a long sip of coffee, coughed and tried the engine again. This time it reluctantly began to fire on all cylinders. The motor roared to life, the irregular pulse pounding the plane and setting all the loose fittings trembling and vibrating.

Geezer tapped frozen gauges and revved the sputtering engine.

Another stream of heavy smoke drifted past, driven in the growling whirl of the propeller's wake. The shuddering plane trembled on the frigid skis, now frozen in the coarse snow. Geezer revved up the roaring engine until the craft shook off the icy grip of the polar ice. The engine thundered, rising in tempo. The metal skis screamed in icy protest as the plane gained speed and began to lurch across the rough strip of ice and snow. Jim sucked in his breath and cinched his seat belt tighter. He balanced the scalding coffee on his knee as the staggering machine gathered speed. It rumbled and bounced across the unyielding terrain until finally it lurched heavily into the air. For a few seconds it seemed to fall again, but the engine gained power, fighting to drag the overloaded aircraft into the frigid arctic wind. The lumbering aircraft gradually eased skyward and began a long slow arc over the endless white terrain below.

Jim looked to the south where the pale horizon had reappeared. From their elevated position, he could see the sun making a vain attempt to color the dusky sky again. He examined the gauges and squinted past the shuddering propeller. The faint horizon was swinging giddily past the cockpit as they pitched around the featureless sky. Jim scowled at the gauges. He could see that about half the instruments were still sitting at zero. The compass appeared to be spinning wildly.

He had logged numerous hours in bush planes and was familiar with the workings of the console. He examined the temperature indicator. His apprehension grew as he realized that most of the gauges were not functioning.

Geezer hoisted his dripping cup to Nester and took a long sip. Nester saluted him with his own and turned back to Jim's tense features. He hailed Jim in turn and Jim numbly raised the container to his lips wondering what the odds of their survival would be if they crashed in this barren wasteland.

The compass seemed to right itself for a moment and indicated that they were heading south. Jim felt a little better. Every minute in the air would put them a few kilometers closer to civilization. He raised the steaming coffee to his lips and took a long swallow. The coffee was black and bitter. The strong brew had a familiar stinging edge to it. It couldn't be! He sipped it again and silently cursed Nester's profile in the dim cabin.

The coffee was laced with rum, strong enough to burn his throat. He drew in a deep breath as the terrible reality hit him. He was heading into the tundra in a broken-down aircraft with an ancient pilot intent on getting himself and his passengers drunk.

For a moment he was overcome with white anger. He had the uncontrollable impulse to strike the two boisterous drunks seated before him. When his anger had cooled a little he directed his rage at the laughing Ukrainian before him. He tapped him roughly on the shoulder and Nester leaned back to hear his words over the thundering drone of the smoking engine.

"Nester," he shouted over the drone of the aircraft. "If we make it down to Yellowknife alive, I'm going to buy two beers. The ones with the long necks!"

Nester raised his cup in salutation and pulled the headset down off his left ear. He seemed, delighted that Jim had finally gotten into the spirit of the flight.

"Then," Jim cursed over the dim in the cabin, "I'm going to take the bottles and beat the living hell out of you!" His words were lost in the roar of the craft as it struggled to remain airborne in the dark sky.

♦ ♦ ♦

## CHAPTER THREE

The darkened craft droned over the endless white landscape, its icy wings trembling in the frigid air, struggling to pull the craft forward. Jim cowered in his cold seat, watching the wing tips flexing under the strain. The plane seemed to be flying in defiance of gravity, plunging and bobbing over rough air pockets while the stressed air frame creaked and moaned in frozen protest. The blunt wings battered their way through the hard air sending shock waves back along the rigid struts and snapping against his hard metal seat.

Jim watched the feeble wing tips fluttering under the strain, then turned away unable to bear the sight. He had choked down the potent coffee, but it had not helped ease the trepidation growing in his soul. Nester had been insistent with his offers to refill Jim's cup, but Jim's angry scowl had finally turned him away. He watched as his companions eagerly passed the thermos back and forth and gulped down the steaming contents. Soon Jim had another concern, for it appeared that Geezer had turned control of the rickety aircraft over to Nester.

Both men were obviously drunk, trying to sing along to some risqué tape playing into their headsets. Jim wondered what might happen if someone tried to contact the wayward flight. He dismissed the concern. The outdated transceiver was probably not in working order.

He peered down at the frozen landscape; a motionless white carpet that stretched from horizon to horizon until it vanished into the gloom. His weary eyes examined the icy panorama, a scene so featureless that at times they seemed suspended and frozen over the barren white plateau. Their craft began to pitch and yaw and Jim clutched desperately at his seat. When the craft steadied again he leaned over and peered cautiously out the frost-covered portal. Jim had flown in the arctic enough to recognize that a storm was forming over the ice packs below. He prayed that their flight would outdistance the fierce winds and that providence would grant them a safe landing. He wondered about their scheduled stopover in Old Bow. Would the plane hold together long enough to reach their destination? Jim stole a quick look at the heavy crates crammed into the compartment behind him, straining against their frail cables with each lurch of the plunging craft.

He tried to imagine the Old Bow airport. He promised himself that if there were an airfield and a hotel at this remote location, he would abandon the flight and take his chances on the next charter out. He knew Nester would be adamant that they continue on together, but he was not prepared to risk his life just to avoid the anger of his feisty companion.

— ♦ —

Three long hours later, subtle changes appeared in the landscape below. Scattered patches of stunted trees had began to stain the featureless white terrain. His companions had grown silent. The thermos lay cold and empty on the floor of the aircraft. Jim watched it rocking on the frigid deck with each pitch of the straining wings. The plane began to lose altitude and they dropped towards the surface of a massive lake. The shoreline seemed to be spreading into a huge V shaped channel. The aircraft continued to wobble lower, the engine sputtering and slowing. Jim prayed that Geezer was the architect of this maneuver and not Nester who seemed eager to gain control of the struggling craft.

Jim watched as Geezer stretched forward, squinting over the console and peering through the swirling snow on the lake, trying to focus his watery eyes on some familiar landmark. The ponderous craft dropped heavily and Jim's stomach heaved in response. He was desperate to get back on solid ground, but he feared the landing even more than his shaky flight under the aircraft's shuddering wings. The savage gale that whipped the storm across the lake reached its angry tentacles skyward, clutching at the frail plane. The gusts buffeted the flimsy ship; allowing it to remain aloft only at the whim of the fierce wind gods below.

They swayed and bounced through the air while Geezer's weeping eyes searched the stormy shoreline. Jim clung desperately to the cold metal seat. Then he spotted them! A scattering of faint yellow lights winked through the storm. Geezer noted the specks of illumination and uttered a triumphant shout as he jammed the rudder, swinging the unsteady craft back over the lake.

His bearings now fixed in his fogged brain, the old pilot began a long slow arc back over the snow covered ice, then rounded the turn. He began to drop the lumbering aircraft onto the lake. Jim was aware of savage winds tearing at the shivering wings, threatening to strip the worn ailerons from the struggling craft. He sensed Geezer's frantic struggle to hold the nose steady against the onslaught of the gale. Jim's senses reeled as they pitched into the swirling snow rising off the stormy surface beneath them. He could hear the fierce cross winds screaming though the taut cables. He had unhappy visions of crashing through the frozen black ice now rushing towards them through the gaps in the storm. He looked at Nester's rigid frame, where the grim looking figure was clinging to his own seat. He would have cursed the obstinate Ukrainian, but his voice was frozen in his throat.

The plane plummeted through the storm and into the heavy blanket of snow raging up from the unyielding lake. All sense of direction or elevation vanished. They were engulfed in the blinding white cloud. Jim felt the cold hand of death upon him and was aware of a sickening falling sensation as the aircraft plunged to its certain doom.

The flight ended with a crashing jolt! The plane began to skid, spinning like a toy across the slick ice. Above the squeal of the aluminum and steel skis, there was a terrible ripping sound as the skis slashed through the snow. Geezer cut the sputtering engine. For a moment a foreboding silence enveloped the night before the craft plunged through a series of hard packed drifts. He heard the renewed screams of the skis on the iron surface of the ice and the protest of the airframe as the stricken machine careened across the lake and tore through ridges of frozen ice and snow. For a few violent seconds the plane bounced and scraped across the rough surface. The spinning craft slowed again as it skidded into a long bank of snow that snapped the racing skis to a rough halt.

Jim was aware of his pounding heart and the silence broken only by the fierce scream of the wind, lashing at the stressed cables. He forced his mind to end its racing course, to analyze his situation. They were on the ground. He had survived the rough impact! He squinted into the night, desperately afraid that he would find flames licking at the thin fabric. There were none, only the muted lights of the cabin detailing the cold cockpit. He mentally checked his stunned body, surprised that all his extremities were still functioning and apparently sound. He strained to focus his eyes into the cockpit where the faint glow from the instrument panel outlined Nester and Geezer, now beginning to converse in normal tones.

"Hey!" Nester demanded. "Did we wreck anything? Can we still take off again?"

Jim peered through an ice-encrusted window and listened to Geezer's vague reply. The sleet was swirling about the downed craft. Occasionally he could see the banks of snow and black ice as the gusts relented. His senses regained their balance and he was aware of the gale howling across the ice. They were down! He was thankful that they had survived, but he took little consolation in their initial success for they were still somewhere on an isolated lake, perhaps a thousand kilometers from the nearest major community.

The occupants in the cockpit before him stirred again.

Geezer cleared his throat and turned to Nester. "Looks like one of them freak storms has blown in. We could be here for a few hours or even days." He cursed and fumbled for his tobacco. "You never know `bout this weather. For sure they seen us come down. They ought to be sending someone out soon," he grumbled. "There's an RCMP constable here most of the time and old Father Baptise, the *know it all* priest. Don't let that yippy old bugger get you alone! He'll try and change your whole life for you."

He made no comment on their desperate landing. Jim wondered how often the old pilot brought his plane down in what seemed little more than a controlled crash.

He watched Geezer fumble for his suitcase. The mittened hands began jamming a few belongings into the battered valise. "I got a friend here that will put me up and the old priest can find you guys a place to toss your bed rolls."

"Damn!" Nester cursed. "We only got a couple of days to get to Yellowknife. How long do you think this weather will last. Maybe I should hike over and make sure they know we are out here."

"Aw, they knows we are here. I'm certain of that. They knew we were coming, probably been watching for days. I can't tell you `bout the weather but I'll guarantee they know we are out here. The sound of the plane will have roused the whole village. No, we just got to sit tight a spell. Someone will be out soon. Someone will come guide us in," he mumbled.

— ♦ —

Jim stretched his aching legs and tried to relax his cold muscles. His chilled body protested the movement and he realized just how tense he had become during their shaky flight. He squinted across the frozen lake again. He needed desperately to go to the bathroom. The snow was swirling past the cracked portals obscuring his vision. Overhead the desolate landscape was lit by the dim light from distant stars. His eyes gradually became accustomed to the faint glow, but all he could see were endless mounds of snow, stirring under the breath of the harsh wind. The rough landing had left him disorientated and confused. He was no longer certain in which direction the shoreline lay or how far away they had come down.

"They don't have a hotel here do they?" Nester knew the answer to his own question. "Or a bar," he added. "Jim, you bring your booze?"

Jim had brought several bottles, but he wasn't prepared to share this information. Maybe this would encourage Nester to moderate his drinking a little. "I brought a couple of bottles," Jim mumbled.

He glanced at his watch. It was 1:15 p.m. Time meant so little up here in this land of endless night. He wondered how long they might be stranded or if the worn aircraft would ever be flight-worthy again.

"Look!" it was Nester's voice piping through the dim cabin, barely discernible over the shriek of the wind and the abrasive hiss of the snow grating across the frozen metal fuselage. "I seen a light moving across the ice."

Jim peered across the windswept landscape, but there was nothing. "Are you sure?" he wanted to believe there was someone out there, but he was reluctant to accept the judgment of Nester's bleary eyes.

"Hey! I seen it plain as hell!" Nester protested. There was a touch of irritation in his strained voice.

For a full minute they peered into the swirling snow until Jim's eyes burned from the strain. Then it appeared, a dull glow, barely visible through the twisting white blanket, swinging like the lanyard on some mystical ship. The faint light moved across the ice to where the wind raged against their stranded craft.

"Yup, you seen something all right!" Geezer began a quick check of his luggage. He seemed eager to abandon his marooned craft. "Someone's come to get us. We'll be warm soon," he chortled.

Two snow covered figures appeared, pale white ghosts, crusted with sleet, only slightly darker than the snow reflecting against the faint gleam of their lantern. Nester forced open his door and a set of broad shoulders pushed thought the narrow opening.

"Hello. Is everyone all right?" the voice boomed. When he verified that the passengers were okay, he continued. "Well, lets get you off this lake and into the village. You could probably stand a cup of hot coffee. What have you got for luggage? Just toss it onto the toboggan and anything that won't freeze, we can take out later."

Jim scrambled down with the others. The lanky stranger had not bothered to introduce himself or the stocky villager accompanying him. That would come later when they were out of the howling winds. Their rescuer was well over six feet tall, clean shaven and lean. The pale lantern revealed the ruddy face and rugged bone structure. Jim guessed from the respect accorded him by his companion that he was the RCMP constable, back from patrol. The man was clad in the same caribou parka as the villager and the uniform, if worn, was not discernible under the heavy winter apparel. Jim tossed his luggage on the sled with the others and followed the constable across the rough ice and swirling snow. In a few minutes they were in the lea of the wind, sheltered from the storm that streamed off the frozen lake. Jim pulled his hood back enough to look around.

The shrouded village seemed to emerge reluctantly from the snow and dark shadows of the stunted forest. It grew in dimension as he squinted into the pale light. The faded log homes blended easily into the surrounding woods and boundless snowdrifts. Even the grey smoke from the chimneys added to the illusion, the thin wisps acting as a willing camouflage that clung to the treetops screening the homes from view. Finally his eyes located a complete village concealed in the sparse forest clinging to the shoreline.

Most of the homes seemed tiny, one or two bedroom log cabins. One large structure stood above the others with a great gaunt cross rising into the dark sky. The faded white paint on the building added to the church's snowy camouflage.

The constable trudged forward leading them towards the chapel where a dim light glowed inside, a faint beacon falling across the darkened snow.

Nester seized his luggage off the toboggan and looked ruefully around the rustic village, before following the constable inside. "Where is that fucking *know it all* priest. I hope he can find us rooms in a hole like this. Otherwise I might just as well sleep in the damned plane. What's the old bugger called, Geezer? Father or uncle Baptized?"

Nester tossed his expensive leather luggage on the frozen planks in disgust and jerked down his hood. The constable set the sputtering lantern on a table and turned up the wick, sending a flickering light across the dim chapel. He pulled his snow-encrusted parka off and began removing his heavy boots. Jim examined him in the glow of the light. He was a big man with a rugged face and a shock of red hair. He looked as if he might be close to fifty. Jim wondered how old a constable might be before he was retired. This man was obviously approaching his pension.

The constable tossed his clothing into a small closet before he turned and extended his hand. "Well, I guess its quiet enough now for introductions. I'm Father Stait. I took over from Father Baptise last spring." He shook Jim's hand with a powerful grip, then turned to Nester. He stepped closer, almost bumping against him, towering over the smaller man, glaring down at the quivering beard and startled eyes.

Nester introduced himself, his voice tight with surprise.

The priest thrust his hand towards Nester. "You may call me Father Bob if you wish, Nester, but please don't call me uncle or insinuate that we are related in any way!" He turned abruptly to Geezer and extended his hand. Jim detected an angry edge in the priest's voice, but it was muted by the faint smile on his lips.

Father Bob moved across the chapel, lighting another lamp. A gigantic Christmas tree emerged from the shadows, the image swelling as the light slowly flared up detailing each decoration on the magnificent pine. The church was sparsely furnished, barely large enough to cram in two hundred battered chairs and small pews. The drab building was decorated with Christmas bows and ribbons. It was obvious the villagers were doing what they could to prepare for Christmas.

"Jim, we have a couple of small rooms attached to the back for guests such as yourself. We'll put you up in one of them. Geezer has some acquaintances that will be delighted to welcome him." He turned to Nester and examined his fierce expression in the pale light. Nester returned his icy stare.

"Yeah, Nester, I think the best place for you would be with old Red Bear. He never uses his spare room except when Brutus visits him. Brutus is an old sled dog, a monster. Hates strangers; especially white men. Keep an eye out for him, okay. Yes sir, Nester, you can bunk in with Red Bear. He was once a chief and a medicine man, but has pretty much retired. He's always home now. I'll take you over as soon as we have a coffee. You speak any Dene, Nester?" He raised his eyebrows and Jim could tell he was enjoying Nester's discomfort.

Nester knew that the towering priest was testing him. He bristled at the man's game, but he just shrugged. "Long as he's got some place to put my stuff. I don't sleep much anyway," he growled.

"Well the old men say this storm will last another two or three days so you may get a little weary before it's over," the priest added.

Jim looked at Nester. Two or three days were unacceptable. Their flight left Calgary in three days for the Caribbean. Jim intended to be on it.

"Did you hear that forecast on a local station?" Jim groped for an answer. "The weatherman back at the base didn't mention any storm."

"Well this seems to be a local pattern. Mostly wind tonight," the priest added. "The old men are a lot better at forecasting the weather than the department. Our short wave quit about the same time we lost our main generator. So my bet is that we will get two or three more days of storm. Were you hoping to be home for Christmas?" he inquired.

Jim explained their plight as the priest coaxed an old wood burning stove to life and pushed a chipped porcelain coffee pot onto the smoking plates.

"Where is the radio?" Jim asked. "Maybe I can get it working." He was anxious to establish communication with the outside world. Maybe they could re-book their flights.

The priest's face seemed to brighten in the pale light. "Well, if you have the skills to repair the radio; that would be a small miracle. There is a real demand for the wireless at Christmas. Everyone wants to send a message and all we can get is static." He rose to his feet and opened the door to an adjacent room. He rolled out a large short-wave radio, connected it to the battery then clipped on an antenna.

"This battery should last for quite a while. Until we get the generator running it's all we have." He flipped a few knobs and the ancient radio emitted a burst of static.

Jim sat down and spun the dials before he flicked it off. "The main power supply is gone. Probably just a blown capacitor. Have you got any spare parts?"

The priest rose quickly to his feet and returned with a small case. He handed the box to Jim. Jim pulled a screwdriver from the tools, removed the cover from the radio and peered inside. "Hey. There it is. A capacitor is blown!"

He pointed to the faulty component and rifled through the box locating a pair of side-cutters and removing the offending element.

He handed it to the priest who eyed the blown component ruefully.

"That's it?" he asked. "And no spares either. Right?"

Jim shrugged. "No, but I can rig one by the time the coffee is boiling. Light me one of those candles. Geezer. Give me the tin foil off your cigarette pack. I'll make up a temporary capacitor. We can stick it together. You don't have any AC for this soldering iron, do you?"

In twenty minutes the radio was pieced back together. Jim turned it on and expertly manipulated the dials. He pulled a screwdriver from the kit and deftly tuned the system. Jim replaced the cover and tapped it gently. A distant voice crackled over the radio.

"There, Father, just like new. You got a good one here. These old babes have been around for a long time, but they don't make them any better. I'll send you a proper capacitor when I get back to base."

Father Bob's face was smiling. "I can't tell you how much this will mean to the villagers. They love to exchange greetings this time of the year and get caught up on the news. Then, of course, there are the hockey pools," he confided. "We even try to broadcast some of the Christmas concerts from the other villages. This is a real Christmas miracle, Jim, thank you."

His face showed his gratitude and he extended his massive hand and shook Jim's solemnly.

Jim was moved by the gesture, but he tried to shrug it off. He looked at Nester's somber face. Nester was frowning and Jim detected a touch of envy. Nester could fix almost anything and he loved the attention this ability brought him.

"I don't suppose you know anything about generators, do you?" the priest asked hopefully. "The department was here about three weeks ago and tried to fix ours, but they left for the holidays and no one knows when they may be back. The village can get by without it, but we really appreciate it at Christmas. They use the power to turn the Christmas lights on and love to watch some of the Nativity programmes on their TV sets." He raised his eyebrows in anticipation.

Nester focused his fierce eyes on the priest. "Hey," he snapped. "I can repair any dammed generator. Who tried to fix it?" he demanded.

The priest returned the shorter man's stare. A look of disbelief crossed his face. "Nester, if you can fix that cranky old generator, then you can call me uncle or anything else for that matter. Would you mind taking a look at it?" There was a condescending note creeping into his voice.

Nester leaned back and sipped his coffee, squinting at the priest. He was in control again. His eyes sparkled triumphantly.

"Yeah, may as well. This rank coffee! Hell, it will probably keep me awake for days. There are some of your spare parts in the plane. Have your guys bring them down!" he ordered. He stood up and carefully zipped up his parka, watching the priest's reaction. "Well, let's go take a look at it. You got tools there, haven't you?"

Jim squinted out the tiny window that graced the kitchen wall. The endless night had reclaimed the frozen wilderness.

The priest called to some of the men gathered around the splendid tree with their children. There was a murmur of anticipation and two of the young men hurried into the night. Their departure started a flurry of activity to secure the spare parts from the aircraft and escort Nester to the generator room. The priest seemed eager to get Nester out to the generator, scarcely able to conceal his delight at the two skilled technicians who had been delivered to him from the stormy Christmas sky.

"Jim, your room is down the corridor." He directed him to the back of the church through a small utility chamber and down a short hall. "This room can be pretty cold. If we get the generator working, we will have some forced air moving from the stove. In the meantime just keep the firebox stoked in the alcove. Some of the heat will gradually work its way down. It also heats the bathroom. The best tub in the village is right next door to you. Please help yourself. It doesn't get used much." He laughed and tugged on his parka.

"Well, I better get my new partner down to the generator shack or he will be calling me names worse than uncle. He seems anxious to work on the old gen set. Not like the last crew we had here. They only wanted to get back to Yellowknife." The priest ducked out into the night and disappeared into the gloom.

Jim tossed his luggage into a corner of the cramped room. He tugged open the small chest of drawers and unlocked the zipper on his suitcase. He peered into the jumbled case then quickly closed the cover. Hardly worth wasting his time. They would only be here for a few hours. He abandoned the suitcase and wandered out into the quiet church. Two older men were lounging before the massive short wave radio. They were surrounded by several bright-eyed children eagerly listening to distant voices in a language that was foreign to Jim's ears. Jim watched one of the buckskin elders pass the mike to a small child. She accepted the device reluctantly, then spoke softly into the machine. Jim marveled at how quickly the news of the repair had swept through the village. More bundled figures were streaming in the door to wait their turn at the crackling set. Every face was smiling and the spirit of Christmas seemed to be descending upon the quiet village.

Jim paused to button up his heavy jacket. Someone turned up the volume on the short wave radio. A familiar Christmas carol in a strange tongue piped merrily into the quiet chapel. The noisy reminder of Christmas turned his thoughts to Tania's missing letter again. He dug out his heavy mitts and jammed his cold hands into the heavy leather. He hurried into the night, eager to escape the memories that were crowding in upon him.

♦ ♦ ♦

## _CHAPTER FOUR_

Jim wandered through the snow-covered village, turning his face away from the gusts; desperate to sweep the cobwebs from his mind. He searched for a singular bright spot in the long day. He knew he should be happy to be alive after the rough landing on the ice, but his thoughts were gloomy and downcast. When the chill of the night had clawed through his warm parka, he headed back to his small cell at the end of the church. The faint light from the stars outlined the chapel. He paused to search for the plane, now a vague shadow, nearly obscured behind the veil of swirling snow. The North Wind's icy chill swept off the lake piercing his warm garments and driving him back to the relative warmth of the church.

His tiny room was an ice box, even colder than his accommodations at the base. He walked back to the stove. Someone had kindled the fire and brought in a mountain of split logs, still dripping their icy cover onto the cool linoleum floor. Jim crammed in more firewood, his numbed hands propped his door open in the vain hope that some of the heat might find its way into his frigid room. He stepped back into the church where a growing circle of happy faces was gathering around the crackling radio.

He watched the scene for a few minutes then returned to lie back on the hard cot, cursing his luck. He examined his sparse accommodations. His room was just large enough to hold the single bed, a dresser, small desk and two chairs. Sparse white walls enclosed him with the image of Jesus Christ on the ivory perimeter. Someone had taken the time to weave a small Christmas wreath around the savior's likeness and the faint odor of pine boughs filled the air, giving the Spartan room the subtle fragrance of Christmas.

He pictured the bustling Calgary airport with the background of Christmas decorations. A sleek aircraft was loading for the Caribbean. He could see the laughing crowd shuffling through the security gates, waving their tickets to sunny beaches over their heads. He shivered from the cold room and the howl of the icy wind slashing against the log walls. He had visions of Nester and himself huddling around a small fire in an icy log cabin, eyeing their empty rye bottles and waiting for the distant spring. He opened his suitcase and pulled out an extra sweater. He wondered how Nester was making out with the generator and if the repair would help warm his frosty room.

Jim stretched out on the firm cot and tried to sleep, but the luxury evaded him. It was not the cold that kept Jim awake. His mind was spinning between past Christmases and the image of the sunny beaches that seemed to fade further away with each lost hour. He slipped off the cold cot and stretched his stiff limbs. He began searching his luggage for the small travel alarm, then quit the task. He didn't know what time it was and it didn't really matter in this land the sun had forsaken. He knew the sable veil of the dark night had returned. He could hear the howl of the wind whistling off the ice packs. The scream seemed to mock him, a reminder they were prisoners in this isolated village. He rummaged through his luggage for the bottles of rye. He was desperate for any diversion to shield him from the memories of the past. They were pushing in again, carried on the faint odor of pine and the glory of the massive tree in the church.

He found a match and managed to light the smoking lantern someone had left on the tiny set of drawers. He examined the bottle in the flickering light. He hated sipping the fiery liquid straight from the bottle, but he needed a drink. Half a bottle of the smooth liquor, layers of thermal underwear and blankets, then perhaps he would be able to sleep away a portion of the endless night.

At least Nester had something to do. Perhaps he should offer to help. He dismissed the thought. Nester didn't need him and probably wouldn't want him interfering. He knew that his partner was as happy tearing down old equipment as he was tossing back cold beer with his friends. The eager helpers the priest had promised him only made the project more attractive, for Nester loved to display his skills to an appreciative audience.

Jim rummaged through all the drawers then abandoned the search for a glass or even a chipped coffee cup. There was nothing. He placed the bottle on the dresser and slipped on an extra pair of socks. He was about to crack the seal when a gentle tapping sounded on his thin door.

The door was already ajar and he turned, expecting to find Father Stait standing in the entrance. Instead he gazed down to locate his tiny visitor. A small girl from the village cowered in the doorway. She might have been six years old, seven at most. She was dressed in high muck-luks and the hood of her parka was crusted with snow. She carried a steaming kettle of tea in one hand and a large tin mug in the other. Jim looked down the hallway. A faint motion in the shadows caught his eye and revealed the figure that had escorted the child through the wintry night.

He examined the girl's wide eyes and somber expression. The tiny jaw was rigid, the rosy complexion glowing from the frosty night. She gazed soberly at his shadowy form for a few seconds and then stepped to the small desk. She placed the steaming kettle and metal cup in the centre of the desk and stood silently by the furniture, but her eyes were frozen to the cold floor. At last she spoke.

"I brought you some tea," she stated shyly, her eyes never leaving the frost tinged tile at her feet.

Jim sat on the edge of the bed and smiled at his young visitor. She was a pleasant diversion in this lonely night.

"Why, thank you. That's very kind. That must have been a long walk in the cold. Was someone with you?"

"My mother walked with me. But I carried the tea myself." Her voice was slow and timid, tinged with the husky accent of her people.

Jim poured a cup and took a sip of the hot drink. It was strong and slightly sweetened. He was moved by her thoughtfulness.

"This is really good tea. Thank you very much!"

"You're welcome," her soft voice answered, but her eyes remained fixed on his stocking feet.

Jim smiled down at her. It had been a long time, too long, since a small child and he had engaged in a conversation. "What is your name?"

She seemed to struggle with the English then answered him. "Little Fawn." Her gaze never left the floor, but he caught her glancing at his feet again.

"Little Fawn. That's a beautiful name. Please, don't be shy. Look up at me and let me see your face."

Her tiny hands reached up. She slowly lowered her hood and looked cautiously into his eyes. The child seemed overcome with emotion. Her gaze fell to the floor again. She crossed herself and curtseyed before him.

Jim looked at the picture of Jesus adorning the room then turned around, searching for a matching image behind him, any likeness that might have caused her show of reverence. There was nothing on the austere white frame.

"Little Fawn. Look at me again," Jim instructed.

She favored him with a quick glance, then crossed herself and curtseyed again. Jim looked back over his shoulder once more, searching for the image of Christ that he might have missed the first time.

"Little Fawn. Why are you bowing like that?"

Her gaze fell to the floor as he waited for her response.

"My grandmother told me, that if ever I met an angel, I should cross myself and curtsey."

Jim paused a moment and then laughed. "Oh. Oh! Hang on here a minute. You don't think I'm an angel do you?" He laughed in amusement. "Somebody is playing a trick on you."

She frowned up at him, her dark eyes were flashing when she answered him. Her tiny voice was insistent, edged with exasperation.

"Father Stait doesn't lie! And you shouldn't either!" she chastised.

"But. But, I'm sure Father Stait didn't tell you that. Surely he must have been joking. Maybe you misunderstood him," Jim stammered.

"No. He didn't tell me. I heard Father talking on the big radio to Brother Lacombe. He told him the Lord sent him two Christmas angels and they landed on the big lake and they were going to fix things up around this place. I heard him plain as *bells across the ice*," the tiny voice insisted.

The phrase rang in his mind for a few seconds. It seemed a very expressive and brilliant choice of words for someone as young as this small child. He searched his mind for an explanation. Jim remembered the priest and the short wave. He knew that Nester was working down at the power plant. That must be it. The priest had been joking with someone on the radio and she had overheard him. He couldn't let this child think that he was an angel. Especially not at Christmas! He stammered for an explanation.

"Maybe he meant someone else! Maybe he was just making a joke about old Geezer or someone with him," he stammered. He almost said my friend, but associating Nester with a heavenly spirit would be blasphemy. He should not be accorded a presence with angels, not by a long stretch. Immediately he regretted his words. He had done nothing to change her mind. Only tried to deflect her attention.

"Geezer is no angel!" she insisted. "He is a drunken old Scottish sot! They should have grounded him when they took his pilot's license away. They should ground him before he kills someone else in that rickety old plane of his!"

Jim felt as if she had hit him squarely between the eyes with a brick. He knew that she had heard this story somewhere. Was it true or just village gossip? Who could have told her this? He remembered the constant smell of liquor on Geezer's breath and the wretched condition of his aircraft. He knelt before the tiny being in the huge parka, desperately trying to comprehend her statement.

"Who said he lost his license? Where did you hear that? Who said that? Has he crashed before? Are you sure he has killed someone?"

He stood up when the absurdity of the situation finally occurred to him. Why was he grilling this small child? He thought of the long flight south to Yellowknife, hours away, over some of the most barren terrain imaginable.

She seemed oblivious to his outburst. He regretted his rash questions and gently patted her bundled shoulder. She smiled up at his gesture and stared reverently into his eyes. A look of pure bliss passed across her face. Jim was moved, it had been years since another human being had afforded him that look.

"Will my grandmother be home for Christmas?" she asked. Her face was alive with anticipation. She smiled and reached out to caress his sleeve. Jim remembered the paintings of cherubs he had known when he was a child; surely if there was an angel in this room, she stood before him now.

"Your grandmother? Well, probably. I don't really know. Well, I think probably. Yea, she will make it home, I'm sure," Jim stammered.

Grandmothers always made it home for Christmas, didn't they?

Her tiny face brightened. "Are you certain?"

Jim hesitated. He felt trapped. What else could he say? She took his silence as a confirmation of her wishes. "Oh thank you. You will make certain she gets home safely, won't you? Will you pray with me for a moment?" Her eyes had become happy lights.

She dropped to her knees. Before Jim could interfere she had begun to pray. Her first words were in soft Dene then she switched to English. She slowly raised her head, glancing carefully up at him to ensure that the Christmas angel who had dropped into her life was receiving her gentle message.

"God, please help Grandma get here by Christmas Eve and bring all the teams home safely. And, God, please, this year have Santa bring mummy something pretty for Christmas. She has been very good and never asks for anything for herself!" She gave her angel an accusing look, as if he had somehow mismanaged this simple task in years previous.

Jim felt the censure in her eyes. A motion at the door pulled his attention away from his tiny visitor. He squinted through the shadows. The priest filled the doorway and a parka-clad woman stood behind him. His timid guest swept over to the woman and whisked out the door. Before she disappeared, she flashed him a quick satisfied smile then scampered into the night, satisfied that she had delivered her important message and a Christmas angel had received it.

Jim rose awkwardly to his feet and watched as they vanished down the hallway. "Boy, that little one has quite an imagination, doesn't she? Who is that child?" He wiped his hands on his jacket as if to brush away her memory.

The priest watched them disappear down the darkened hallway then slumped down on the solitary stuffed chair the room offered. Jim noted that he had put on his white collar. The neatly cropped red hair, black shirt and collar afforded him the formal appearance Jim expected in a priest.

"That was Little Fawn and her mother. The mother married a white prospector working up here a few years ago. But the marriage didn't last. He didn't find his fortune and he soon left. She has been through some difficult times. She won't accept any charity either, just allows us to give her enough to make sure her daughter is taken care of." He pushed his hand deep into a coat pocket. "By the way, I have a small gift for you. I hope you will accept it. It's a little carving I picked up on the coast. This is Christmas and I want to thank you again for repairing the radio. I can't tell you how much it means to our village this time of the year!"

The priest placed the soapstone carving on the table. "Are you comfortable here? Is there anything else I can get you?"

Jim was more flustered than touched. He wished he had something to give the priest in return. He remembered the two bottles of rye he had placed on the small bureau. They were still in gift-wrapped boxes. He heard himself stammer.

"Oh, thank you, Father. Thank you very much! I was just going to bring something for you. I hope you like Alberta rye." He snatched a package off the dresser and thrust it at the lanky redhead in the white cleric and heavy fur parka. The absurdity of his gesture suddenly registered. He felt like a damned fool offering a priest at bottle at Christmas. He was certain that the good father would decline the gesture and he breathed a sigh of relief at the priest's answer.

"I can't really accept your gift," the priest returned. "I seldom take a drink anymore, except on very special occasions or when I'm coming down with a cold."

He turned the bottle slowly over in his hands. "Alberta rye. The world's finest rye..." he murmured and cleared his throat. "I used to drink this on occasion in my younger days." He examined the bottle again. "Perhaps I will accept your generous gift. My throat has been a little tender." He rose from the chair, his rangy frame filling the small room with his presence. He started for the door, the bottle partially concealed under his jacket.

"Good night and Merry Christmas, Jim. If you are here much longer, I hope you will make plans to join us for Christmas mass."

"Father," Jim hesitated. The question was still there. "Does the saying *bells across the ice* mean anything to you?"

The priest laughed and sat down again. He examined the bottle of rye. Perhaps he wanted a taste now. "So you have heard of the legend already have you? The locals here have a belief, and I think it rather a beautiful one. It goes like this. If you hear the bells ringing across the ice, it is a sign of good luck. Now this means only the sound of the bells, not the mushers or the dogs barking. They don't usually put bells on their dogs. They are hunters, but at Christmas it's a tradition they follow. Even the dogs sense that it's a special time. Teams will bark and create a lot of noise when they first start to run. When they have been running hard or are a little tired, sometimes you can hear the bells from a great distance. The sound carries for miles across the ice where there are no trees to deaden the sound."

The priest seemed eager to talk and Jim felt the need of a drink.

"Father, I too have a tender throat. I was about to take a little medicine. If you can find a couple of glasses, I'll invite you to join me."

The priest stood up. The bottle was still in his hands. "I will join you, Jim. First there are a few small matters I must attend to. It would be pleasant to talk to someone who has spent time down south. Ten minutes. And I'll bring some glasses. Perhaps even ice. It's a common commodity around here," he laughed.

Jim watched as he ducked through the doorway. He opened the small bureau and rummaged around until he found another pair of heavy socks. The now familiar smell of the pine boughs seemed heavier tonight. He remembered the tiny pine wreath Christine had given him when she was still in Brownies. She had made one every year after that, even when they had resorted to an artificial tree. He had learned to appreciate the piney scent. It had become a Christmas tradition, meaning a little more each year. Like Tania's lengthy letter to him now.

He cursed the post office again; surely it was the mail service that had lost the precious letter. He leaned against the bureau, picturing

Christine and Tania's radiant faces. Damn! He was daydreaming again. He picked the jug up, tempted to take a swallow from the bottle, but he stopped himself.

He was relieved when Father Stait returned with two heavy whisky glasses and a pitcher of ice cubes. Jim noted the priest had not brought any water to dilute the potent brew. Good!

He poured the liquor slowly into the priest's glass, giving him ample time to protest and stop Jim from over filling his glass. The protest never came. When Jim had dribbled four generous ounces over the cubes, he stopped and poured himself a matching drink. He picked up the glass and raised it to the priest. He noted that the white collar had been discarded.

"Season's Greetings, Father."

The priest raised his own glass. The drink seemed to fit comfortably in his huge hand. "May God bless, Jim!" He tilted back the mellow liquor and took a long swallow. "Aw. Nothing smoother than pure Alberta rye," he stated. He raised the glass again and casually drained the remaining spirit. He banged the empty tumbler back on the table. Jim would normally have taken this as an invitation for a refill, but he hesitated. The big man was, after all, a priest. Just to be on the safe side he finished his drink, being careful not to gulp the mind numbing grog. He raised the bottle to the priest, a silent offer to pour him another generous shot.

The priest did not respond, but he rang another ice cube into the glass and sat back. Jim flooded the ice and refilled his own glass, thankful that he would not have to pace himself with a temperate priest.

"So you have not been up here long, Father?" Jim felt better. The familiar warmth of the rye was already loosening his tongue. "What brought you up to this God forsaken part of the country?" Jim inquired.

"Jim, it's rather a long story. A wearisome one at best, perhaps when we have a little more time I can bore you with all the monotonous details. But a priest is supposed to be a better listener than a talker. Tell me what brings you into this wondrous land of ice and snow?"

Jim hesitated. It was Christmas. Perhaps the priest could help exorcise some of the demons that tormented his soul. He hesitated, he did not want to relive the memories, not tonight! "No, I don't have a very interesting story to relate either, Father. I guess one reason I wound up here in the North is that some people feel that I'm not a great conversationalist."

The tall priest leaned carefully back on the protesting chair. He took a long swallow of his drink. "Well, we do have a long night, but I'll give you my Reader's Digest version." He reached for another ice cube and Jim could see him preparing the story in his own mind.

"I didn't ask for this transfer and it certainly was not in my vocational plans," he laughed a little. "No, it was not part of my original career path. They ordered me up here. At the time I probably had one of the best parishes in the world. Ever been to Philadelphia? There was loads of money in the parish and the church was always packed. We lacked nothing. I lived in a converted mansion, did fundraising, celebrity marriages and generally mingled with the rich and famous. Some people say I can carry a fair tune." He paused and smiled at the memory. "I was even receiving voice training from some of the best teachers in the country." He paused and finished his drink.

Jim raised the bottle and when the priest made no attempt to wave the offer away he poured another generous shot into his glass.

"Yes," he laughed. "It seemed I was headed for the top. A lot of powerful people had me penciled in for the Vatican. The scotch was free along with most everything else. Some people like to tempt a priest it seems." He looked over his glass of rye at Jim and Jim listened for the censure in his voice. The reproach was not there.

"I succumbed to the pleasures of the bottle and other delights that are unbecoming to a dedicated man of the cloth." He took a long swallow and Jim watched while the memories flooded in on him.

"When my superiors learned of my failings, there was talk of disrobing me. Other priests have been punished by banishment into the wilderness. Someone must have felt that this was the best path for me. But it turned out not to be a chastisement. I found something here I had never known before. I found true peace and I found that I can really contribute. Not as a traditional priest. Heavens, no! These people are as pure as anyone on earth. Here I'm more of a social worker and a teacher. I attend council, help instruct, take minutes and keep the bridge open to the outside world. I tell them about Christ if they want to listen and, surprisingly, most of them do," he swirled the rye in his glass. "And, so here I am."

There was a gentle rap at the door. A woman from the village appeared. She smiled shyly at the priest. The Father excused himself, promising to be back in a few minutes. Jim sat staring into his glass. The priest had told his story quickly. He had not dealt with any details. Jim found himself trying to fill in some of the blanks. He finished his drink, then poured another. The smooth rye had untangled the anxious knot in his gut. He felt the gloomy ghosts of Christmas lifting from his tense shoulders.

In a few minutes the priest returned. He leaned back in his chair and swirled the ice cubes around in his drink then turned to Jim. "Well you have heard my story, perhaps someday you will tell me yours. Just curious, Jim, are you a Catholic?"

Jim hesitated. He did not want to offend this imposing yet gentle pastor. "No offense, Father, I quit believing in God and even Christmas a long time ago. I don't believe there is a spirit world. The only ones that touch me are here," he tapped the bottle. "I'm an engineer and a scientist. I can't help the way I think."

His blasphemy did not seem to offend the lanky cleric.

"Jim, when you have been here a few days you may have some second thoughts. If the spirit world is alive anywhere, it's alive amongst these people. I have seen many things manifested here that I can't explain and I doubt if an engineer and a man of science could either. I don't think anyone should give up on Christ. I believe there are only two types of people. Those who have found the Lord and those who are still searching. Maybe you are still searching."

Jim shrugged; the priest's words did not hold any significance for him. "Well, that may be, Father, but I've never seen anything that I couldn't explain. Anyway I don't expect to be here for mass. I'm sure the weather will break and we can get out. I'm certain you will have a great Christmas without us."

"Yes, they will have a great Christmas. I don't doubt that. They still know the true meaning of the season and they know how to keep Christmas. The village is a little anxious right now. Several of the men are out with the teams and no doubt this storm has halted their travel. A few of the sleighs have gone to the post at old Fort Simpson."

"Christmas shopping, even up here, Father? Commercialism has reached into their hearts too, has it?"

"Well, Jim, you may just have a point," he laughed. "It has become a tradition. They will pick up a toy for each of the children and perhaps a few gifts to repay others for their kindness. There will be candy and even the odd turkey, although that special bird is little more than a curiosity up here. They have a strong preference for caribou or venison. Each year at this time, some of the teams go out for fresh meat and some do go to shop. The hunters returned with all the meat they could carry. But the trip to Fort Simpson is three days one way. They would not try to travel over the lake in this weather. They will be sheltered now in some small line camp, waiting out the storm."

Jim finished his drink. "Little Fawn and her mother, they will receive gifts, too, won't they?"

The priest sat silent for a long moment. "Yes, Little Fawn will, but her mother would not want her to receive to much from the community."

Jim remembered Little Fawn's request to him. "Her grandmother, will she make it in for Christmas?"

The priest looked at him, surprised at his knowledge of the child's grandmother. "Her grandmother is not well. She is with a small band in a winter camp. The site is many hours ride away by dog team. She visited Little Fawn and her mother last Christmas. I doubt she will be in this year. The trip would be too much for her. Where did you learn about the child's grandmother?"

Jim shrugged; he remembered the girl's happy face when he had promised her that her grandmother would be with her for Christmas. He felt badly, but what could he do? He took another sip, hoping the whiskey would help rationalize his dilemma.

"Father, it's just something I heard somewhere." He looked at the bottle. It was half-empty. He poured himself another shot and raised the bottle to the priest. This time Father Stait shook his head.

"No, I've had more than I wanted, there are a few chores I must complete before I turn in. Thank you and good night." He rose and stretched the stiff muscles in his back. He paused for a second in the doorway.

"Jim, keep your heart open and remember, even old Scrooge eventually discovered Christmas."

"Yeah, sure, Father. When I get down to Martinique, perhaps I'll look again, but the ghosts of Christmas that I meet are the same ones each year. They are there to torment me and I don't think they are going to offer me redemption."

The priest hesitated in the doorway. Jim waited for his parting comment.

"Good night, Jim. Pleasant dreams."

Jim searched for the bottle of aspirins. He swallowed three and washed them down with a generous shot of rye. He listened to the howl of the wind whipping the course grains of snow against his walls, reminding him that the storm was still his captor. He pulled the cold blankets over his head and drifted into a fitful sleep.

♦ ♦ ♦

## CHAPTER FIVE

Jim struggled through the whisky-gray fog numbing his mind, trying to orientate himself in the darkness and the intense cold in the unfamiliar room. Somewhere in the distance a disturbing drumming pounded at his dazed senses, regular and persistent, an irritating discord that commanded him from his rest. Someone was tapping on the door of his tiny cell. His first concern was the time, in this land of perpetual darkness. He staggered up, trying to locate his watch and the source of the irritating noise. A pale glow at the door caught his attention and he squinted into the dull yellow light. The faint gleam from a flashlight revealed Nester's bearded face.

"Hey! Are you going to sleep all bloody day? I heard you got it pretty cushy here, with your own private suite and all," he examined Jim's sparse accommodations and chuckled to himself before turning away.

"Where does that bloody priest keep the fucking coffee. Old Red Bear don't drink coffee and my nuts are washing away in watered down tea!"

Jim's shivering fingers managed to light the tiny lantern on his bureau. He examined his watch under the sputtering flame. It was 8:35 a.m. He could hear the incessant howl of the wind slashing off the lake. Behind Nester's parka clad figure, the hallway seemed as black and cold as the night itself.

"How is your place, Nester? Pretty rustic, eh!" He had some compassion for his companion, shoved in with a grouchy old villager by the indignant priest. He was certain Nester was sharing a small cabin in the most primitive of conditions.

"Ah, it ain't that bad," the shaggy beard mumbled. "The old chief cooked me a fantastic steak for breakfast, about this thick." He held up his hand, but Jim could not distinguish his fingers in the darkened room.

"Hey! It was one of the best I've ever eaten! Must have been about two pounds and juicy as hell. Old bugger doesn't say a word though, guess he don't speak no English." He turned and left Jim struggling into another layer of clothing. Jim could hear him rattling around in the cupboards next to the stove.

"Geezer is coming over," Nester shouted over the clatter of the pots. "Our old plane landed in one piece. He has to repair a damaged strut on one ski. No big deal. If the weather clears we may get out of here today."

There was little conviction in his voice, listening to the ghostly howl of the wind and dismissing their chances. Still, Jim probed Nester for some positive news.

"The priest thought the storm would last for another day or two. Do you think it's breaking up?"

"The wind is changing. Geezer figures there will be some quiet periods by evening. Geezer wants the moon in the sky so he can see to take off. We only need a few minutes to get off the ground," Nester reminded him.

"Plane's half buried, so some of the men from the village are going to help dig it out and pull it around to face the lake."

Jim felt a little better. There was a ray of hope after all. He joined Nester and stoked the smoking fire, pressing close to the glowing plates to warm his shivering body. "How did you make out with the generator?"

Nester poured his coffee and took a noisy sip of the steaming brew. "Hey. Those guys from the department! They're a bunch of incompetent assholes. There are grounds on two coils. All they did was put in a new control system. Idiots! One of the bearings is misaligned on the motor. We worked on it till 2:30 a.m. this morning but, it's going to take another day to get everything going. The crews are coming back to give me a hand at nine."

"Too bad," Jim muttered. "If the weather clears today, you won't get finished."

"You know we might, if we had another day," Nester grumbled. "These guys haven't had that fucking generator working properly since last June. What a shop they have here. Equipped with everything. We might still finish in time."

"Nester, did anyone say anything about some of the kids calling us Christmas angels?" he asked, trying to keep his voice level.

"Yeah," Nester chuckled, there was a note of approval in his voice. "I seen a couple of them following me around and trying to walk in my tracks. You know there's no one here who could fix that cranky fucking generator!" he probed Jim for a compliment before continuing.

"They said it hasn't run properly since it was installed. Just staggers along for a few hours, then trips out." Nester finished his coffee. "Well, guess I'll head back to the gen room. Geezer could use a hand with the plane."

Jim watched Nester hurry into the cold. The conceited technician did not seem concerned that they were being mistaken for angels. Jim had the unhappy feeling Nester was willing to perpetuate the myth. He listened to the howl of the wind again and prayed for an early release from this confining village. He remembered the promise he had made to a little girl who wanted to see her grandmother home for Christmas. The ailing grandparent was trapped in a bush camp hours away. He didn't want to look that kid in the face on Christmas morning.

Jim crammed more wood into the rosy stove, desperate to drive the chill from his shivering frame. He heard the church door open and felt the pull of the wind sucking the precious warmth from the tiny alcove. Geezer's snowy figure appeared, followed by a crowd of smiling villagers, eager to help free the snow bound aircraft.

Geezer gulped down a coffee, wiped his soiled mittens across his chin and shuffled silently into the darkness, trailed by the bundled figures from the village. Jim watched them troop along behind the graceless old bush pilot then he reluctantly pulled on another layer of warm clothing and followed them to the downed aircraft.

— ♦ —

In a few hours they had shoveled a short runway over the ice and swept the stranded craft free, wrestling the chipped propeller into the gale that stormed off the lake. When the bone-numbing task was complete, they trekked across the frozen village to a small feast prepared by some of the women. The weather and the struggle with the unwieldy plane had given Jim a ravenous appetite and he devoured the tasty meal with relish.

A constant stream of admiring visitors filed through the door. Most stayed only a few minutes, long enough to share a cup of scalding tea, then smiled at their guests and disappeared back into the endless gloom.

Jim had the uncomfortable feeling that many of the villagers were bringing their children to gape at him and old Geezer. He felt as if he were on display, for the youngsters treated him with a respect that bordered on reverence. The tiny faces peeped around their mother's swaddling clothes and stared at him with the same sense of wonderment he had found in Little Fawn's eyes.

Geezer gulped down his last cup of tea and commented dryly on the parade.

"You know I been in a lot of places and been treated a lot of different ways, Laddy. But this is the first time anyone ever judged me in the company of angels. You and Zary sure don't look like cherubs to me and I heard enough stories about that little Ukrainian chauvinist to write him off as a seraph. Kind of makes a feller stop and ponder his ways, don't it now, Laddy?"

Jim looked into the wind burned face and bulbous nose. He was in no mood to discuss angels. He mumbled a thanks to his hostess and struggled into his heavy parka. She was still smiling when he and Geezer shuffled into the darkness.

An expectant hush had fallen over the snowy village. Jim looked to the motionless treetops. The harsh wind had died away, only the occasional gust stormed out of the north, whipping a frozen cloud of snow across the distant lake.

"Think you could take off in this, Geezer?"

The ancient pilot examined the sky. "I've taken off in worse and got away with it, Laddy. We need to wait for the moon is all. Got to see where we is headed. Some of my instrumentation don't work too good in this here cold weather." He jammed his numb fingers into his pockets and fumbled out a twisted pack of cigarettes. Jim waited until he had lit one. He walked along beside the hacking figure as Geezer battling for breath against the sting of the tobacco in his violated lungs. Jim looked to the darkened sky for any sign of the moon, wondering if the old pilot's tired eyes could distinguish between a good runway and a poor one....

The silent church was nearly deserted. Jim examined his watch in the faint light from the flickering lanterns. It was only 5:30 p.m. He knew the moon would not be over the horizon for several hours. He glanced around the tiny chapel again. The tree seemed brighter, fuller than before, swelling magically under the gracious hand of Christmas. Small children were adorning the great tree with additional decorations each time they visited. One of the elders was removing the ornaments from the lower branches and passing them to his assistant balanced on top of a crude stepladder. Jim watched as the young man secured them to the upper branches.

He remembered how Christine and Tania had loved to pile decorations on the tree. He fought the closing memory and thought of pouring himself a stiff drink. Perhaps the mellow rye was not a good idea. If they were to attempt a takeoff soon, he wanted a guarantee that at least one member of the crew was sober.

He dropped his parka in the cold bedroom, then fled the tiny cell. Jim searched the darkened church, looking for the old pilot. He found him at the back of the chapel. The worn figure had removed his heavy toque and was seated piously in the last row. His bleary eyes were fixed on the image of Christ outlined in the dim light over the pulpit. Jim wondered what thoughts might be running through the decadent old pilot's mind and what personal ghosts he might be battling from his lengthy string of Christmases long past.

Jim slumped into a rough seat and examined the small sanctuary again. The familiar sound of carols drifted in over the short wave, driving him back to his room. He collapsed on the cold bunk, aware of muscles he had pushed to the extreme digging out the aircraft. He pictured the plane and the rocks they were boiling in battered 45-gallon drums. The hot stones were a crude, but effective method of warming the frozen engine. Old Geezer's predictions on the weather seemed to be holding, for the constant moan of the gale had subsided to a soft sigh. The moon would soon be over the horizon. Jim visualized the old Norseman lifting him into the quiet night with his tickets to the sunny beaches clasped in his hand. He began to imagine the smell of wet tropical gardens and the salt spray from the warm beaches.

The scent of the small pine wreath teased his nostrils as he dozed under the warm comforters. Then the ever-present spirits began to shoulder in again, their dark forms casting ominous shadows over the images of the white sands. Once, many years ago, all his images of Christmas had been glowing and warm. He tried to remember when the spirit of Christmas had begun to fade away for him....

It still had substance during his stint in the Air Force, the night they had walked down to the parliament buildings in Ottawa and listened to the carillons playing Christmas carols. The magical feeling was still there at midnight when he had phoned his parents back on the frozen prairies. It was alive and well in his college years when he had driven home through the falling snow to spend Christmas with them two years later.

His drowsing mind led him back to one special night long ago. It was the evening before Christmas Eve. The magic of the season was still there. It was the first Christmas that he and Anne realized they might soon be spending their holidays alone. Tania had begun dating and both she and Christine had hinted that they were going out with friends on Christmas Eve. He knew it bothered Anne now that the girls had boyfriends and were more interested in spending Christmas with their schoolmates than the family. It bothered him too, but he had the smooth rye to blunt the growing ache.

Anne had moved onto the couch, cuddling close to him, wanting to talk. When she found him sullen and unresponsive she had retreated to their bed. He had followed and soon felt her warm hand on his shoulder. He lay there for a moment, tempted to turn and take her in his arms. He knew how passionate she could be. Even now the thought of her lovemaking brought a flood of warmth to his loins.

The sound of a car pulling into the driveway had caught his attention. He heard Tania calling to Brandon, their huge shepherd. Jim was relieved that she was home early and he listened as she left the kitchen and hurried up the creaking stairs to her room. He lay rigid under Ann's warm hand until she withdrew it....

Was that the night that the spirit of Christmas had begun to slip away? The night the girls began moving towards womanhood. The night he no longer responded to Anne's need for a friend and a lover.

It seemed that ever since that evening long ago, the true meaning of the season had begun drifting beyond his reach. For a time he had fought desperately to recapture it, but it had been like trying to grasp a vapor.

He tried to remember some of the little things that had once made Christmas special for him. Shopping for the children's toys, the sound of carols on the car radio and the falling snow against the Christmas lights. The flame of Christmas warmth had flickered on occasion, but it had never re-ignited again. Then it was gone!

He would wake up with a thundering head and plod numbly to the kitchen for a coffee, realizing that Christmas had passed him by again. The departing season left only the dreary memory of missed opportunities, gone like the bright Christmas bows he had discarded into the battered trash can.

He snapped upright on the firm cot, banging his stocking feet onto the floor and grabbing for his warm boots. He was determined to escape the remembrances that were flooding the tiny room. Pouring a cup of hot coffee he hurried past Geezer, still sitting silently in the last row. He slumped down a few seats away. Geezer seemed lost in his own private memories. He did not acknowledge Jim's presence.

Jim sipped the coffee and looked around the silent church. The pain of the lost Christmases was still there. He tried to fix a blame to it. Surely someone had stolen the magic from him. He heard approaching footsteps. He realized Nester was standing beside him!

"Hey! What are you guys doing? You and Geezer look like a couple of old monks. You bastards taking up religion?"

Jim rose quickly to his feet, trying to shake off the hard memories. Geezer stirred in his cold pew. He looked guilty. Guilty of being caught in a church, silently praying for things he felt he didn't deserve.

"How is it going, Nester? You have any luck with the generator?" Jim asked, hoping to take Nester's attention away from his own somber countenance.

"Hey! Almost running. I replaced the main bearing. Cleaned up the rings. Set all the pole pieces. It should run like a charm. Just have to dry it out some more. The insulation is still damp. The stator is full of frost. I got the crews putting stoves in there. A couple of shifts and the unit will be warm. Then we can start it and set up the controls."

"Two shifts, Nester!" Jim shook his head. Nester was setting up shifts; organizing everything around him, just like he did back at the base. He appeared to be enjoying himself.

"We'll be long gone!" Jim insisted. He looked at Nester's lined face. He knew his hard-driving companion had hardly slept since they had landed, but there was something else in his weary expression. Nester appeared completely relaxed and a strange inner peace seemed to light his countenance. Jim didn't like it. The look didn't fit the fierce Ukrainian!

Nester glanced at him then quickly focused on the towering tree. "Come on! Priest wants to see us all. Says he has a favour to ask. Maybe he wants us to line him up with a horny broad," he chuckled.

Jim rose to his feet, feeling better. Nester was starting to sound like himself again.

He followed Nester and Geezer to the priest's office. He still didn't like the expression on his companions' faces. They had the manner of eager choirboys, anxious to please their minister. When they walked in, the priest greeted them warmly. Two elders who smiled and nodded at their guests accompanied the cleric. Jim was suspicious. One of the villagers began to pour steaming cups of tea. They offered the hot cups around. This was not a chance meeting. Jim could sense they had something important to discuss.

For a minute they exchanged pleasantries and then the priest began. "The elders think there will be break in the weather for a few hours," he looked uncomfortable and gulped his tea. "I expect that you may want to leave as soon as the moon comes up, but...."

Jim shivered at the sound of the *but*; anything except a hasty departure was completely out of the question.

The priest fixed his eyes on Geezer. "There is an old woman waiting for a chance to visit our village for the holidays. This may be her last Christmas. We were hoping you could pick her up and bring her in before you fly south."

Geezer returned the priest's stare. There was no sign of emotion on his weathered face, only a look of bliss as he gazed reverently at the priest's chaste white collar.

A stiff hand swiped at the dripping red nose. He stared down at the floor before scratching the thatch of gray hair on the back of his rough neck. Jim knew the old Scotsman had a reputation for being cheap, a man who would milk nickels every time the opportunity presented itself. He waited for Geezer to name his price. Jim was certain it would be exorbitant enough to discourage their interest.

"Well, if you was to give us some of that aviation fuel you got in your store house, enough to top up our tanks before we leave for Yellowknife, that would about make it square. Where is her village?"

Jim wanted to protest! Anything could happen during the flight! What if they damaged another ski? What if the decrepit plane froze in on some isolated lake?

He watched helplessly as Geezer scratched the stained gray beard forming on his craggy chin. "I'd need one of the lads here to come along in case we freeze into the snow after we land." He cranked his stiff neck around to Nester. Jim waited for Nester to put an end to this insanity. He knew that he would find a reason if they turned to him.

Nester gave an indifferent shrug. "Yeah. I guess we could. You got enough gas?"

Nester seemed to be falling into the cunning priest's trap.

Geezer scratched his stubbly chin again. "Maybe we should bring out one of the barrels and top her up." He squinted at his shattered wristwatch, shook his hand and tapped the cracked crystal with a blunt finger.

Jim watched in dismay, wondering if anything the old pilot owned was in working condition. Nester silently raised his own lean wrist and pulled back the heavy sleeve on his parka, exposing the expensive timepiece to Geezer's watery eyes.

"Well, I guess if we was to pull the petrol out now, fuel it up and run her for a few minutes to make sure the gas is good. She would still be warm by the time the moon come up. The lads have been heating the engine, so she should fire up okay. Want to give me a hand, Nester?"

Nester shrugged into his parka as Geezer squinted at the rough map the priest had sketched for him.

"Jest that small lake on the river is there? I didn't even know there was a village out that way," Geezer muttered.

"No. There is no village, but the elders have arranged for a team to meet you on the ice where the river forms a delta. Do you think you can find it?" the priest rapped the crude sketch with a pencil.

Geezer's watery eyes focused on the rough drawing. He pulled a bent pair of spectacles from his pocket, one lens was cracked. He squinted through the other glass and traced a shaky finger over the outline. "I found tougher places with less than this." He jammed the paper deep into his pocket and struggled into his parka. Nester pursued the hunched form into the arctic night.

The elders had followed the conversation with obvious satisfaction. They finished their tea, smiling at the priest. Jim slumped back, trying to control the frustration boiling up inside him. The old men accorded his grim features a quick nod and hurried after Nester, delighted to assist in the fueling of the ancient Norseman.

Jim sat stiffly in his hard seat. He had visions of the plane disappearing into the gloom, leaving him stranded in the remote village.

Father Bob stretched his creaking arms over his head in what was becoming a familiar motion. He smiled at Jim. "Your friends are very magnanimous. Are you sure you wouldn't like to go along. It will be a beautiful evening when the moon comes up."

Jim shivered at the thought. "Father, how did you do that? Geezer has a reputation for being the cheapest, most miserable old bastard in northern Canada. And Zary, it's not like him to volunteer for anything."

The priest smiled again. He seemed satisfied with his accomplishment.

"Jim, I have acquired some knowledge of human nature over the years. One of my original career objectives was to be a personnel manager for a large corporation. Might have worked out. Who knows? Now you take old Geezer. For years he has been hauling corpses down south, overcharging the government, and flying without proper documentation. He probably has a list of sins longer than...." he struggled for the words, not wanting to condemn the old man. "Well, longer than many of us. He hasn't been near a church or a priest in a good many years. He was once a good Catholic, too, I'm told. And at his age, every time he hauls another mortal remains south, you can bet he considers his own mortality. Maybe he wonders how soon he may be riding in that back seat himself. Now, here he is, stranded in Old Bow with time on his hands, walking into a church and meeting a priest several times a day. He gets an opportunity to put a few points on the board for his side. Well, it's nice to have a servant of the Lord marking your score card." He smiled at Jim. He appeared eager to continue the conversation, but Jim was in no mood to oblige him.

"You understand people pretty well," Jim snapped. "Did you ever think you might be using him?"

"No! No, Jim." He stood up and spread his arms to the sky. Jim knew he was putting on a performance for his sake, but he was not impressed.

"Hallelujah!" the priest sang out. "For a few hours he is just a tool of the Lord! Bringing in an ailing grandmother to see her family. The gas is government and shall tax him nothing. And praise be for the rest his failing kidneys are receiving."

He looked at Jim's stony face and dropped the exaggerated facade. "Besides, I told you there might be some Christmas miracles taking place up here." He raised his eyebrows waiting for Jim's response.

Jim shook his head. "Father, all I see is a damned, manipulative, old priest holding up my departure for the Caribbean. But I've got to ask you this. The old woman they're going after. Is she Little Fawn's grandmother?"

"Well I ain't really that old, Jim, but yes, indeed. I believe an angel promised the child that her grandmother would arrive home in time for Christmas. So we had better deliver, hadn't we!" He leaned forward in his chair hoping again for a reaction from Jim.

"Father, you have to do something about that kid," Jim shot back. "She thinks we're angels and you're not doing a damned thing to show her differently!"

Father Bob stretched his aching back again. It was obvious that he was enjoying Jim's discomfort. "Well, you know angels are pretty hard to define, Jim. Even the Bible is not that explicit. They have been known to come in all shapes and forms. Who am I to destroy a little girl's faith." He poured another cup of tea and grandly offered the pot to Jim.

"You're a priest, for God's sake! You're supposed to tell the truth!" Jim shot back.

"Yes, but how can I be certain. By the way, you did promise that little child that her grandmother would be home for Christmas? Tchh,

Tchh, Tchh," the priest chided and grandly sipped the cup of tea.

"Well, no. I didn't. Not exactly."

"Her grandmother is very special to that little girl. Are you saying you don't want to be part of making her Christmas wish come true!"

Jim sat back on the cold chair fixing his eyes on the Yule wreath behind the priest. He could not feel anger or disappointment. A few extra hours wouldn't make much difference. He was still concerned about the window in the weather. If it didn't hold, they could miss another chance to escape. Still, he couldn't begrudge the plane trip, not as long as he did not have to venture into the dangerous icy sky.

"Jim, you look a little shaky. Could I offer you a drink?" He pulled a bottle from the drawer. Jim recognized the package. It was the gift-wrapped bottle he had given Nester for Christmas, back at the base. Nester had not even bothered to remove the nametag.

"Present from a visiting cousin of mine," the priest laughed. He reached over and poured Jim a generous shot.

Jim accepted it with a shaking hand. The priest raised his cup of tea and took a long swallow. "You know, Jim, what I miss most here? This might surprise you. I miss someone to differ with. The Dene are a very diplomatic nation. You couldn't start an argument with them if you wanted to. I used to debate at University. I don't suppose you would be interested in debating some contentious issue now, would you?" the priest laughed. "I must have said something to offend you."

"Father, you have said lots of things this evening that offend me, but I'm still not in the mood to argue."

"No, I understand that, as an engineer and a scientist, you really believe that you can explain everything you encounter, don't you, Jim."

"Yes. I do, but I don't want to argue over that either."

The priest poured a generous shot of rye into his tea and favored the cup with an appreciative smile. "Very well, it's no fun arguing with someone who does not wish to contest issues of controversy. Besides, I still believe that before you leave here you might change your agnostic engineering mind."

Jim leaned forward, a response boiling up inside him. Then he saw the delight in the eyes of the huge red head. He would not give him the satisfaction. His anger was dampened as Nester swept back into the room.

"Shit!" he announced. "Old Geezer has more help now than he knows what to do with it. There is no reason for me freezing my ass off out on the lake. I'm going back and grab a couple of hours sleep before we take off," he chuckled. "Got to rest up for all those horny babes down south. Hey, you guys having a drink? I could use a good shot. It always helps me sleep." He was already extending his cup towards the huge hand with the bottle.

Father Stail eyed Nester for a long minute. "You know, Nester, at your stage in life you should be looking for a stable relationship. Not chasing everything that wears a skirt."

"Hey!" Nester sneered, "what does a damned priest know about women and relationships. I was married for close to 20 years!"

Jim thought he could see the hint of a smile on the priest's face as the huge hands poured a stiff drink and pushed the heavy mug across his cluttered desk. "Sit down, Nester. I think you need a little guidance from someone who knows more about women than you might think."

Jim swallowed his drink and rose unsteadily to his feet. If the priest wanted someone to argue with, he had picked the right person. Nester would contest any issue. The priest might be a skilled debater with several university degrees, but he had never had to pit his skills against anyone as sharp as this quick-witted Ukrainian.

"Nester, I'll go see how the dry out is going on the gen set. Have a nice friggin flight across the pack ice!"

Jim hurried through the church zipping up his parka, trying to remember the last time he had been warm. There was a small knot of people clustered around the short wave radio. For a moment he felt a sense of gratification for the happiness he had brought them. At least he would be leaving them a small Christmas present. Probably one of the first ones he had not put on his credit card in many years. He passed the towering tree again. There were several wide eyed youngsters gathered before this magnificent symbol of Christmas, admiring the decorations on the splendid pine, sniffing its pungent odor and pointing to the Christmas angel at its apex.

He examined the happy faces of the children and remembered how much he had loved the smell of pine boughs when he had been a child. The picture was part of a past he did not want to relive tonight. He hurried into the cold, anxious to avoid the depressing memories that were crowding in on him again.

Nester had directed him to the generator in a remote corner of the village. Brilliant stars lit the faint pathway leading past the small cabins. The golden glow from their lamps painted shining panels on the blue surface of the pristine snow. He approached one small log structure with a flickering candle and wreath in the window. Something in the scene made him pause. The breeze was hushed, barely a whisper through the surrounding forest. Even the great pines stood in silent awe. The cabin was newer than most, the logs the color of fresh wheat straw, mounded over with new snow and contrasting against the dark pines bowing in the background. It was a scene from a post card. He found himself thinking how much the scene would appeal to Anne. For a moment he wished there was someone here to share the picture with him. He cursed under his breath and hurried away, angry for letting the scene beguile him.

He followed the power lines, singing in the chill of the night and they guided him through the brush to the steel frame of the gen shack. He could see two black stovepipes jutting through the snowy roof, expelling a stream of smoke and red sparks into the frosty night air.

An unfamiliar sound made him pause. He was certain he could hear music over the sigh of the dark pines. Perhaps his mind was playing tricks on him. He paused on the narrow pathway and his ears strained against the low moan of the wind in the distant evergreens. Somewhere in the distance, carried on the frost of the night air, the sound of an old fiddle cut cleanly through the forest.

The mellow sound drew him under its spell. Jim was easily captivated by good fiddle music and his ears were starved for melodies after their isolation in this remote village. The sound seemed to be coming from the squat metal building that housed the gen set. He did not recognize the tune, but he had never heard a waltz played so sweetly on a fiddle. He guessed they were amusing themselves while they tended to the heaters and the gen sets. For a moment he considered turning back to his tiny cell so as not to interrupt their diversion. The icy draft cut through the woods, reminding him of his half-frozen condition. He shivered and hurried forward, forcing the protesting doors open and stepping into the room.

He could see several faces turning towards him in the dim light of the cold chamber. The lamps reflected on their swarthy skin and the whites of their eyes stood out against the dark background and frosty walls. The old musician was dressed in tattered jeans and a faded, blue, denim shirt. A contrasting red bandanna was knotted about his sinewy neck. The minstrel did not appear to have noticed Jim's entrance, and continued to play, totally absorbed in his sweet music.

Jim slammed the door behind him and searched the darkened room. Nester had set up two stoves, converted oil drums with chimneys and air intakes from outside, one on each side of the gen set. Two young men were heating cinder blocks on the stoves, then stacking them against the units. The hot bricks created a warm environment around the generators, despite the mounds of frost that edged the corners of the building. Jim strolled over to the nearest stove, removed his mitts and spread his fingers to receive the warmth.

Despite the roar of the glowing furnaces, the building was still cool. The cold air did not seem to bother the occupants who had removed their outer garments and were happily avoiding the rosy stoves. A smiling face presented Jim with a comfortable chair and he settled self consciously into the seat adjacent to the smoking oil drum.

He huddled against the welcome heat. Perhaps he could finally get warm. A pair of mittened hands removed two smoking cinder blocks and exchanged them with cooler bricks. Jim shivered as the first song ended and a carol began. The talented musician was playing *Silent Night*. He had never heard it played more beautifully. Jim looked at the worn fiddle, marveling that such an antiquated instrument could create such exquisite music.

As his eyes grew accustomed to the darkness, he counted twelve members in the small group, including a child sitting dreamily upon an old man's knee next to the faded fiddler.

When the music started again they chose to ignore Jim, leaving him to soak up the welcome heat and relax in the dim room. He looked around the sparse Quonset hut. The flickering blue flame of two coal oil lamps, turned low and emitting just enough light to allow the workers to move safely about the darkened room, illuminated the darkened building. The red flames flickering though the cracks in the makeshift stoves added a dancing crimson tinge to the darkest shadows.

Jim checked his watch. It would be two or three hours until the moon rose, another couple of hours until the plane returned. With a little luck they would be in the air, headed south, by midnight. They might still be in Calgary tomorrow in time to catch the afternoon flight to the golden beaches of the Caribbean.

He pictured himself in the tropical paradise, in time for the rum to ease the sting of another bachelor Christmas. He wondered if he would have time to call Tania or if she would even be home. Where would she and Christine spend their Christmas? He had not intended to cut his schedule this close.

He thought of Tania's missing letter again and how he intended to chastise his thoughtless daughter for the wayward gift that held his last faint hope for a cheerful Christmas.

The frayed bow danced across the worn strings, quivering though several jigs and polkas, then the fiddler begin to play *We Three Kings*. It took him back to a Christmas concert with the kids when they were still in Regina.

After the recital he had helped them wrap their presents for Anne. Anne loved Christmas more than most kids. Another box under the tree could always make her smile. She would pick up the new addition and try to guess what it might be. She had the annoying habit of shaking the gaily-wrapped presents. He remembered how she loved to get Christmas cards and how she enjoyed shopping.

She would start her excursions as soon as the Halloween candy had been put away, eagerly seeking out the malls that had the audacity to exchange their Halloween displays for nativity scenes on the first day of November. Anne's shopping had been one source of their conflicts. She was always buying things, particularly at Christmas, spending more than they could afford. It had made him furious at the time.

Now it didn't seem so bad. She'd never had much and the child in her sometimes overruled her better judgment. Anne seldom shopped for herself. The shopping bags were always crammed with presents for everyone else.

He remembered the packet of canceled cheques that he still carried in his wallet, cashed by Anne and Christine. It wasn't much of a substitute for a lost wife and daughter. He would pour over the pieces of paper with their recent signatures on them, trying to find a message in the cold canceled documents. Had Christine carried them in her wallet for long or cashed them immediately? Did she have enough money or was she depriving herself just to get by? Was her hand trembling? Did the signature slant upwards indicating that she was in a happy frame of mind? Jim stood, trying to shake the hard memories that were rushing at him in the winking light of the fire and on the music of the carols.

The heavily mittened hands appeared again and shifted more warm blocks. Jim shuffled awkwardly around the crude stove, finally warmed by the roaring fire. He checked the cold electrical generators. The primitive heating system seemed to be working. There was no trace of frost on the heavy steel frame. They would be dry to the core in a few hours with the warmth and low humidity of the gen shack.

Jim moved from the comfort of the warm fire and waved a quick goodbye to the cluster of smiling faces. He stepped back into the brutal cold of the night without a word of farewell to the small group. He was surprised when he looked at his watch. Two hours had slipped away under the magical spell of the Christmas music and the flickering lights from the primitive stoves.

The distant stars were still shimmering against the velvet blackness of the night sky. The pale, frozen moon was cautiously creeping over the distant horizon. The cold bite of the North had again locked its jaws on the tiny village. The dark night seemed silent as a frozen tomb. He hurried through the frost, listing to the creak of his heavy boots on the frigid snow. Just time to toss his possessions into his waiting suite case. The snow-dusted plane would soon be in the air again.

♦ ♦ ♦

## CHAPTER SIX

Jim slapped his frozen mitts together, hurrying to reach the church and the relative warmth of the silent sanctuary. He pushed through the doors, skirting the shimmering tree and the small assembly, equally divided between the crackling short wave and the silent splendor of the great pine. He hurried past the priest's simple office where Father Stait and Geezer were reviewing the rough map under the flickering kerosene lamp.

"Jim, thank goodness you're back," the priest called to him. "We were going to send someone for you. Nester can't make it. Geezer needs you to go along with him."

Jim started to sputter. This was impossible! Nester had volunteered to go. Why couldn't Nester make the flight?

"Yes, I'm afraid he got a little carried away with the rye and lack of sleep. We practically had to carry him to Red Bear's cabin. We got into a rather stimulating discussion about Nester's life style and values." The priest chuckled at the memory.

Jim spun around and stormed across the snow. "Let me see if I can wake the bastard up. He is probably just playing possum," he snarled. Nester would enjoy sending him into the wilderness while he slept off a few drinks.

He raged along the snowy path to the tiny cabin, silently cursing his hard drinking colleague. Damn him! The son of a bitch had made a covenant with a priest and a little girl who thought they were angels. Now he was trying to stick Jim with the obligation! He would shake the cocky Ukrainian from the liquor-induced stupor. Drag his hairy bare balls across the rough ice until Nester screamed himself awake.

He pounded the door open and charged into the small bedroom. Nester was sprawled across a narrow bunk. His heavy flannel shirt was open, exposing his hairy chest. He was snoring loudly and the smell of booze hung on the crisp air like a sour vapor. Beside him on the cold bed was the largest husky Jim had ever seen. It was Brutus, the husky the priest had warned Maurice to avoid. The snow-white coat was a dead giveaway. For a moment Jim froze, expecting the dog to attack. The old sled dog who hated white men. The hoary killer that had a tendency to snap at strangers was cuddled contentedly against Nester in the frigid room. The dog's massive head was over his lap. The imposing creature appeared totally at ease with the stranger sharing his bed. Nester's left hand was twisted into the powerful dog's mane. The giant husky appeared to outweigh Nester by at least 15 kilos.

"Zary, get your God Damned lazy ass of that fucking bed," Jim cursed.

Nester answered with a snore and a drunken grunt. Jim guessed that he had consumed the best part of a bottle of rye. The man had hardly slept for close to 48 hours. The husky lifted his enormous head from Nester's sleeping body. The powerful dog raised one corner of his black lips, revealing a set of imposing teeth. It was the most subtle of motions. Jim examined the burning eyes and the huge fangs under the dark lips. This husky was incredibly old, but he had faced down howling blizzards and once a pair of northern wolves had backed away from his determined stand. Jim was only a passing inconvenience.

Jim seized Nester by the foot, the anger driving him to jerk the exasperating drunk off the comfortable bed. The dog was on his feet in an instant. All the teeth were showing now and a deep rumbling growl was coming from somewhere in that gigantic throat. The giant husky meant business!

Jim released Nester's sock. The foot bounced back on the firm bed like a lifeless piece of firewood. The dog's black lips slowly relaxed over his teeth. Nester grunted in his sleep and the dog turned, raising a concerned ear to his inebriated companion now mumbling through the shaggy beard.

"You bloody, arrogant, little sot," Jim cursed. "You and that great ugly cur. You're two of a kind. You've both seen better days and you both still think you can whip the entire bloody world. You work for 48 hours straight, gulp down a bottle of my best whisky and then you wonder why you're near dead. And now I've got to climb into that rickety old plane with your drunken partner and risk my ass while you're sleeping off a gigantic hangover."

Jim shook his fist at the sleeping figure. The powerful husky slowly raised his lip again, exposing the horrible clenched teeth.

Jim pulled up his hood and shivered. He knew who would be making the cold flight into the wilderness with old Geezer.

— ♦ —

The spent engine sputtered a few times, then barked to a reluctant life in the crystal air. Geezer jammed levers and tinkered with switches on the battered panel. The engine backfired and then stalled. He cursed the cranky machine softly then hit it again. This time it spun with more purpose, the prop biting into the heavy air, blue smoke whirling past the cockpit. For a minute or more Geezer revved up the sputtering engine, then apparently satisfied, he applied full throttle. The plane began to shudder and creep across the snow-covered ice. Soon it was bouncing wildly over the unforgiving iron surface, drawn forward by 300 horsepower of smoking pistons and whirling prop. Jim held his breath. By the time he began to breathe easier again, they were in the air, heading towards the cold light of the distant North Star.

Geezer's watery eyes located the frozen river a few miles up the coast, a smooth dark sash snaking away from the lake and into the endless white wilderness. He swung the creaking plane in a slow looping arc, no sunlight to guide them, only a thin cold moon and remote starlight. Jim marveled at the brilliance below. It didn't take much light to illuminate the landscape. The crystalline snow reflected and amplified every speck of available light. Their eyes soon became accustomed to the faint silhouettes of the pine-covered hills and the meandering river. After forty minutes they soared over a large channel where the current widened into a lake.

Geezer maneuvered the lumbering craft over the frozen reservoir, frowning down at the barren landscape. There was no sign of activity below, not even a campfire. Jim wasn't surprised. Geezer shrugged and his shaky hands guided the stuttering plane down. It skimmed over the surface, landed lightly on the snow then glided to a gentle halt. Jim felt a touch of admiration for the old man's skills as Geezer cut the smoking engine.

There was no sound on the snowy expanse of the lake, only the creaking of the skis pressing into the snow and the pop of the brittle wings settling back on aging struts. Geezer pried a protesting window open and the crisp air flooded in, overpowering the smell of smoke and warm oil in the cabin. The nearest shoreline was over a kilometer away. The tiny lake was surrounded by a range of low hills, crowned with black pines that threw ominous dark shadows across the sparkling snow.

"Shit," Jim cursed. "I need a leak." He stepped out and relieved himself. The silence was even more remarkable outside, only the occasional distant ping of the ice, yielding under the relentless bite of the frost. Geezer joined him and stumbled around the battered plane, his watery eyes examining the rigid struts and taut cables that held his aircraft together. Jim watched the windshield wiper mitts swipe at the runny nose.

"How long you gonna wait?" Jim asked

Geezer shrugged again. "Seems kind of strange, don't it, Laddy? This is where they said she would be. We are in the right spot for sure," he mumbled.

"Yeah," Jim scoffed. "How the hell would she know we're coming? The radio?" Jim cursed, "or maybe the welcome wagon lady dropped in for a fucking spot of tea and left her a little note on the cupboard with her basket of goodies."

"I've seen stranger things out here," Geezer muttered, blinking into the night.

Jim squinted across the expanse of glistening snow, listening for any sound in the absolute silence, half expecting a pack of snarling wolves to descend upon them. The cold stars seemed near enough to touch. The northern lights flickered in the distant sky, but their dancing splendor held no attraction for his callused soul.

"It could be a nice spot if it weren't so friggin cold. Can you find your way back?" He did not want to be lost in this barren wasteland.

Geezer snorted an unintelligible answer and Jim hoped the derisive response was in the affirmative.

"If this weather holds, we could leave tonight. Eh?" Jim asked, hoping to draw the old recluse into a conversation.

Geezer cleared his throat, but he did not respond.

Then Jim heard the sound, somewhere in the distance. The excited bark of the dogs. "God! Don't tell me," he gasped. But, it was a team! They were coming fast, from the far end of the lake. Slowly the black dots materialized against the shimmering snow. The team was racing along the shore in a wide arc as if searching for some anticipated rendezvous. Then the black shadows swerved in their direction. Sure enough, the dogs began to bark in unison. He could hear bells ringing across the snow.

"Well, no luck tonight," he muttered, drawing only a curious glance from Geezer.

The dogs dashed across the lake, barking in excitement at the smell of the plane and strangers now wafting towards them in the frigid air. The musher shouted his commands and the surging team glided to a halt in front of them. The driver was a big man. He roared again and the lead dog dropped in the snow. Jim could see passengers stirring amidst the pile of furs and quilts heaped upon the slender sled.

A vaguely feminine form moved awkwardly from under the cover of the blankets and struggled towards them. She stumbled though the knee-deep snow, short and stocky, so bundled up in the great caribou-skin parka that Jim was not certain if she were indeed a woman. At first Jim guessed she was Eskimo, but she approached Geezer and pulled back her hood.

"Hi, I'm Angie. I'm with old Kaneeta. Do you have room to give me a lift to Old Bow?" Her words were in perfect English and the voice was feminine and sensuous despite her dumpy appearance under the layers of clothing.

Geezer snorted, "Hell, we got plenty of room."

Jim tried to view her face in the faint light dancing across the distant sky. Her pale image could best be described as plain. In the soft glow of the familiar stars, her face appeared oval and pale with the soft features of a teenager. Still, he guessed she was close to forty. She turned to Jim and smiled. It was a nice smile, honest and friendly. Jim felt very comfortable with this pleasant stranger.

"Hi!" she gushed and extended her hand. "I'm Angie." She shook his hand through the layers of mittens. "Kaneeta is really quite feeble. I'll have Toekkay lift her into the plane. We have a couple of small bags with us. Can you put them on board?" She laughed softly, delighted at the chance to gain a flight to the distant village.

Jim watched her in the pale light. It had been a long time since he had been close to a white woman.

They squeezed into the lone passenger seat in the back. Jim was aware of her ample hips against his body. He watched as the old woman was hoisted up and strapped into the front seat.

Geezer secured the doors and began flicking switches in the cockpit. Jim looked down at Angie. She was smiling again, her eager face was visible even in the muted lights of the dash. He put his arm around her shoulder as the two of them pressed together under the common seat belt. She laughed and snuggled closer. Her warm breath caressed his cheek. It was sweet and inviting. He caught the scent of her faint perfume. Despite her plain features he felt a rush of desire stirring within him.

"Jim, I really appreciate your giving me a lift to Old Bow. They have a radio there and I can call my office. I was supposed to get a flight out a couple of weeks back. I'm a department nurse and there was a sick child in the camp. The agency must have left without me by now and I had no way of contacting them."

"Didn't the priest radio your camp that we were coming?" Jim was certain he must have misunderstood her.

She laughed into his puzzled face again. "Oh, no, it's just a small camp. They don't even have a transistor."

"How did you know we were coming?" Jim demanded.

"Oh, the Old People told me the plane would land on the lake. They just seem to know these things." She continued her nervous prattle as the engine revved up for take off. Her voice was melodic and sweet, but Jim was looking out the window to the departing sled gliding back across the ice, disappearing into the boundless wilderness as mysteriously as it had arrived. She cuddled against his chest and spoke softly to him, but her words were lost in the sputter of the trembling engine. He moved his head lower and she breathed into his ear sending reluctant shivers up his spine as she clasped his arm.

"It's not a long flight, is it? I'm really a very nervous flyer. I prefer the dogs." She laughed again, apparently delighted to have his company.

Jim was aware of the warm female at his side. He wondered what it would be like to try and make out with her under their layers of clothing in the cramped seat. She seemed to invite his flirtations. Despite her plain looks and plump body he found her strangely appealing. She clung to him as the plane lurched across the snow and struggled into the air.

Jim looked out the window. He could see the dog team racing back into the night, a flowing shadow moving comfortably through the woods. The plane droned on across the snow-covered forests. Jim pressed his knee against Angie, aware of her warm hips even through the layers of clothing.

The old aircraft began to shudder. It hit an air pocket and dropped heavily in the thin air. Jim clutched desperately at the frozen seat! For a few seconds they seemed in an endless free fall towards the frozen surface of the lake, now rushing up at them from the gloom, then the struggling craft bottomed out and sputtered forward. All thoughts of Angie's warm body were driven from his mind. Jim would be grateful for a safe landing back at the isolated village.

♦ ♦ ♦

## CHAPTER SEVEN

The quavering Norseman droned through the silence of the arctic night guided by the unchanging North Star and Geezer's faltering hand. The thin moon dipped towards the horizon, enticing long black shadows from the silent timber and onto the trackless snow. Jim's spirits were soaring. The air was calm and Geezer's tough old fingers appeared steady, firmly in control of the reluctant craft. The worn engine was running smoothly. Visions of the warm surf swam before Jim's eyes. He was pleasantly aware of the soft female at his side, but she was only a pallid reminder of the seductive women he anticipated in the crowded bars and on the golden beaches of the Caribbean.

He stole a glance at Angie's serene features, outlined in the dim lights of the cabin. How could anyone remain feminine and perfumed in this land of endless frost and isolation? He wondered what might have happened if the two of them had been marooned in this remote village for a portion of the long arctic winter? It didn't matter really. He would be aloft by the time she had unpacked.

His imagination was leading him down sensuous paths when the finicky Norseman jarred his thoughts back to reality. The wobbly craft began to shudder and his queasy stomach warned him of a rapid descent. He clutched the seat in panic, then breathed easier when he realized Geezer was buzzing the faint lights of Old Bow. He could see the dim outlines of the buildings. Faint yellow patches of light stood against the black pools the capricious forest had painted along the lake. A swirling red bonfire danced on the ice, a lively beacon created by the village youth, more an excuse to hold an impromptu party than a flare to guide the returning plane home.

The falling aircraft creaked into a slow turn and then plunged towards the black surface. The plane dropped heavily and jarred to a rough landing on the ripples of snow patterned by the wind across the frozen lake.

Angie clung to him with the intimacy of a lover until the skis glided to a stop and the creaking wings drooped back against the protesting struts. Jim's ears were instantly tuned to the silence of the cold night. He breathed an audible sigh of relief. The air was calm and serene. The fierce gale had faded into the distance.

A swinging lantern started across the ice. A sled was already on its way from the church. Willing hands helped them down from the plane and gently settled the old woman into the pile of warm blankets and furs. Angie covered Kaneeta's frail form with a robe then turned and called to Jim.

"Kaneeta wants to present you with a small gift and express her thanks, Jim. Would you ask Geezer to come over?"

He called to Geezer and they moved reluctantly over the snow to the frail bundle on the sled. Jim was eager to collect his gear and load the plane for Yellowknife. He had no time to waste in meaningless thank-yous, but he could see no way of avoiding the pointless ritual. The old woman was nodding and smiling. She seemed happy to be free from the frightening shudder of the aircraft and back to the village of her daughter. She extended her bare hands through the frost of the night and Jim felt obliged to remove his own mitts and expose his flesh to the bite of the arctic night. The old crone seized his fingers and brushed them against her frail lips, all the while muttering in Dene. She pressed a coin into his palm and then performed the same ritual with Geezer. She was still smiling and nodding when Angie tucked the blanket around her and the sled bumped its way across the rough ice.

Geezer watched them disappear in the direction of the church. He slammed the twisted doors and gave the battered skis a ritual kick before turning to Jim.

"Well, I've had some poor fares in my time, Laddy," he muttered, "but this is the first time anyone ever paid me two bits." He laughed and spat rudely onto the snow.

Jim examined his coin in the faint light from Geezer's failing torch. It was an old Canadian 25-cent piece, worn and smooth with use. It felt incredibly warm despite the chill of the evening. Jim guessed that someone had placed a hot water bottle in the old woman's blankets. He dropped the coin into the liner of his mitt determined to keep the small token. Perhaps he could have some fun with Nester over the meager tip. His high sprits had returned and he no longer begrudged his obstinate partner the hours of sleep that he had stolen.

Geezer chuckled again "Well, Laddy, if we get about 17 more of these; I know a great spot in Old Town where it will buy me a large pint of draft when we reach Yellowknife. Let's grab our gear. Maybe Mr. Zary will buy me that steak he's been promising me at The

Prospector."

Jim hurried after him, anxious to rouse Nester, collect his waiting luggage and get under way. His sensuous visions of Angie were replaced by slender bikini clad women frolicking on the sunny beaches.

They had only started along the snowy path to the church when a distant sound piped across the lake, freezing them in their tracks. It was a hellish whistling discord, far out on the ice, like the lashing of a thousand tiny whips. Geezer scowled across the rough surface and scratched the stubble on his battered chin.

"Christ, Geezer! What the hell is that?" Then Jim felt it, the first desperate fingers of the touch he dreaded most.

There was a faint moan in the nearest pines, a gentle sway in the uppermost branches. The cold hiss of an icy wind sounded against the taut fabric of the old Norseman's wings. Then he saw the wintry front swirling across the black ice. A low cloud of snow slammed against the startled pair, like the wash from some ghostly titanic propeller. The edge of the village was instantly engulfed in the snow and wind.

"Damn it!" Geezer cursed. "Where the hell did that come from? I got to get back and haul tarps over the plane before she fills the engine with ice. Let's duck into the church till I find some of the lads to give me a hand."

Jim plodded mechanically to the church door. He paused outside and sheltered his eyes against the onslaught. He watched the faint silhouette of the old Norseman disappear behind the swirling white cloud. Jim shouted an angry curse into the teeth of the gale. It seemed to relent a moment, startled by his violent challenge, then the winds lashed back with renewed fury. In a minute the plane was swallowed by the hungry storm. Once again they were victims of the swirling snow that had held them captive for the past two days.

Jim staggered into the church and collapsed onto a rough pew. He knew he had been beaten!

Inside the quiet sanctuary, the placid Christmas tree and flickering candles seemed unmoved by the raging blizzard again slashing off the black surface of the lake. The tranquil scene began to calm his stormy thoughts. He sucked in a deep breath and removed his frosted glasses.

Angie's gentle face swam into his vision. He could see her smiling at him in the dim light of the candles and the smoking kerosene lanterns. She appeared younger in the pale glow of the church lights. Her laughing eyes seemed larger, her lips fuller. She might have been attractive with a little make up and some fashionable clothing, Jim mused.

Angie moved towards him and placed a warm hand against his chilled flesh. He flushed at the touch. Her hand was puppy soft, warm and inviting. For a moment Jim forgot the slash of the frozen ice crystals against the logs of the church, the bitter disappointment of the missed flight. This woman was nothing special, but perhaps she would provide a diversion if they were confined to this isolated village for a few more hours. He knew she was waiting to meet with the priest and receive her billet, but she seemed in no hurry to leave his side.

"Jim, have you heard them sing?" Her voice was hushed, almost reverent. She seemed caught up in the spirit of Christmas she had found in this simple church.

Jim replaced his glasses and focused on the scene at the opposite end of the chapel. The frost was fading from the edges of his icy lenses. He recognized Father Stait, facing a tiny semi-circle of children, the eldest no more than twelve. Their dark eyes were following the priest's every motion, peering reverently over the lighted candles they held in their tiny hands. Jim knew they were preparing for the recital on Christmas Eve. The concert was tomorrow night, the day before their flight left Calgary!

He tried to brush the disappointment from his mind by concentrating on the scene emerging before him, swimming into view as the frost retreated from his glasses. The first two rows of the rough-hewn pews were filled with the children's parents. With them were the younger brothers and sisters, watching in expectant silence and waiting for the music to begin again.

Jim squinted into the shadows. The ancient fiddler he had seen singing and playing in the gen room stood against the great tree. He was dressed in a bright red flannel shirt that contrasted with the emerald needles of the great Christmas pine. The bow was poised in his hand and the glowing redwood of a magnificent violin was tucked under his weathered chin.

The priest nodded to the minstrel and he drew the bow over the quivering strings. The first notes fluttered to the rafters, like a flight of nightingales released from the depths of the magical instrument. Jim squinted into the flickering light. Was this the same forlorn musician who had played carefree tunes on a ravaged fiddle back in the red glow of the gen room?

The melody from the strings still resonated through the church as the priest lifted his head and began to sing. His voice was magnificent, an incredibly smooth baritone that filled the tiny church and overpowered the hiss of ice crystals surging against rough-hewn logs. The power and beauty in the priest's voice soared with the violin. His song touched a chord in Jim's soul that he had thought long buried somewhere deep in his cynical past.

*"Silent Night!"*

It was merely two words, hardly even a sentence, but the notes seemed endless. Jim recognized the voice of an ultimate professional with a range far beyond his expectations. Before the echoes had faded and Jim's spirit had lost the emotion created by the condensed line, the priest nodded to his tiny choir and their beautiful soprano voices responded. Their music was in perfect harmony and Jim soon understood that a gifted professional had coached this tiny choir.

"*Holy Night!*"

Their voices soared, the brilliant notes carried higher on the lament of the mellow violin.

"*All is Calm!*" the priest crooned. The violin trembled to a higher pitch, the notes struggling to match the rising baritone until the small soprano choir could respond.

The exquisite harmony flowed through the tiny church, touched Jim's soul and misted his eyes. He remembered how the spirit of Christmas had once moved him beyond his powers of description.

He felt Angie brush against him. In the enchantment of the music, her hands had moved gently into his own. Now their fingers had become intertwined and her warm hands filled his.

He tried to speak, but his throat was locked.

"Have you ever heard anything so beautiful?" she breathed. Her voice was little more than a whisper in the hush of the dim cathedral. Jim looked down at the cold floor and tried to brush his own emotions aside.

Surely it was the disappointment of the missed flight; the tension of the past days causing this unfamiliar tug at his heart. He heard the priest dismissing the youthful choir and watched as the towering figure moved down the aisle and introduced himself to Angie.

"Let's all go back and have a coffee in the office. I have asked some of the children to bring old Pocanta. She'll be delighted to find a spare bed for you, Angie. We are very glad to have you. I hope you can find time to spend Christmas with us."

Angie was radiant. Jim wondered what sort of isolated bush camp she had come from that made this rustic village so appealing.

The priest turned and led them to the rooms at the back of the church. "Well, Jim, I see you were able to bring Little Fawn's grandmother back before the storm returned. No trouble finding her Geezer, tells me." He was smiling at Jim, testing his reaction again.

Jim followed him into his cramped office. He did not reply. There was something puzzling about the way the team had found them on the isolated lake. The storm's mysterious abatement and sudden return still troubled him. He did not intend to concede his bewilderment before the triumphant smile of the towering priest.

"Yes, Father, the flight went very well. Geezer seems to carry a great deal of luck with him. I expect that he acquired it after half a century flying in the bush."

His refusal to acknowledge anything unusual did not appear to bother the lanky priest.

"Aw, yes, luck. Luck will explain a lot of things. Particularly to an engineer and an educated man of science like yourself, Jim. Anyhow, let's have that coffee. Geezer tells me he found a can of condensed milk in his supplies. By the way, the wind seems to have picked up again. This change in the weather didn't catch old Geezer off guard, did it? Not after half a century of flying in the bush." He tossed the phase back at Jim and raised his eyebrows awaiting his reaction.

Jim did not make any comment. He accepted the coffee and watched as Angie scribbled a note for her supervisor in Winnipeg. Jim examined her face in the flickering lamplight and tried to guess her age again. She was smiling and telling the patient priest all the details of her time in the small winter camp.

Jim was tempted to invite her along to Yellowknife in the old bush plane! She would make a pleasant seatmate on the long flight. The thought was a passing one. He let it drop. She seemed in no hurry to abandon this remote village.

When she had secured the priest's promise to relay her message on the short wave, she smiled at everyone and bid them a good night. Jim returned her warm smile. Her eyes were those of a young girl eager to flirt and he found himself studying her departing figure as she hurried out into the darkness.

The priest stretched his cramped muscles and turned to Geezer and Jim. "Well, gentlemen, I'm afraid you will have to excuse me. There is a young couple who have asked to have their baby baptized this evening. Their cabin is only a couple of hours south of here. I'll probably get a little sleep after the baptism and the celebrations. So, I may not see you until morning. One of the men from the village is coming along with me to exchange Christmas gifts. He is an excellent driver. I guess they don't quite trust me out there alone, even with a seasoned team," he conceded. "The trail is sheltered so if you want to see some great country, Jim, you're certainly welcome. The northern lights are dancing tonight and the sleighs are running empty. I know the family would consider it an honor if you or your companions attended."

"No, thank you, Father. Racing through the bush at night in a frozen sleigh is not my idea of a really good time."

"Very well then. I'll be on my way. Perhaps you can keep an eye on the stove. Our young nurse has asked if she can use the bathtub. I've left a boiler of water heating on the firebox."

Jim thought of Angie, bathing in the room adjacent to his. There was something erotic in the image. He imagined himself spying on this most private of activities. The idea seemed inappropriate in the small church, with the image of Christ gazing down upon him. He tried to dismiss the picture from his mind.

The priest began packing an expensive black leather attaché case. The briefcase seemed alien to this remote village, a prestigious bit of luggage from somewhere in his past. Jim marveled at the man who had adapted so quickly to this savage land. He pictured the distinguished redheaded priest mushing through the bush and wondered what his blue-blood parish back in Philadelphia would think if they could see him in his coarse caribou parka.

Jim finished his coffee and reached for his mitts, then he felt Geezer's iron grasp on his arm!

"Your coin, Laddy! The money the old woman gave you! Show it to me!" His voice was brutal, demanding, edged with shock. Jim looked into the mad eyes of the eccentric old bush pilot, then at the priest. He was thankful the clergyman was present. Their aging companion seemed completely mad.

Jim jerked his arm away from the man's iron grip, but Geezer was insistent.

"Where is your coin, Jim? Where did you put it?" his voice seemed edged with fear.

Reluctantly, Jim reached into his bulky mitten. He had dropped the token between the warm liner and the coarse outer leather shell. He searched for the coin. He was not even certain it was still there. He had not placed much value on the old woman's trifling gift. His cold fingers located the quarter. It was still warm to the touch, despite the pervasive chill that seemed to penetrate every portion of this village. He pulled the silver piece out, but his eyes were locked on the Geezer's grim features and his outstretched trembling hand.

He extended the currency to the mad bush pilot, hoping that his motion would quench the fire in the old man's wild eyes.

His maneuver seemed to work. Geezer compared the coins and a look of relief flooded his tense features. Jim glanced down at the coin that had caused all the excitement. The token seemed brighter now, emitting a rich copper glow in the gentle radiance of the priest's lamp. Jim looked closer. There was something puzzling about the coin! Then it struck him. It was the color. It was not copper. It was gold! He dropped the quarter on the inkpad. His confused mind refused to believe what his eyes were telling him.

Geezer reverently placed his own shining coin beside Jim's.

"Gold!" Geezer gasped, his words were barely audible over the snarl of the wind, gnawing against the frozen logs of the church.

"These are newly struck, one quarter ounce gold coins from the Canadian mint. An hour ago they were only worn quarters and we both witnessed it." He turned to the priest.

"Mother of God! Father! How did she do it? Are we witnessing a miracle?" He dropped to his knees to examine the coins, then crossed himself in an almost forgotten manner.

Jim snatched his coin off the table and held it to the faint glimmer of the lamp. He reached back into his mitt, searching desperately for the original quarter. The mitten was empty!

"Angie!" he gasped, struggling for an explanation. "It must have been her! She must have switched them. She must have done it while we were listening to the choir. Geezer, she must have swapped yours, too!" he stammered.

He paused and turned to the priest. His mind was grasping for an explanation. "The light from the plane, maybe it was just too dim. Maybe we didn't notice!" His voice trailed away. He knew they had been given 25-cent pieces, despite the poor light.

"No! No." Geezer insisted, his voice had grown calm compared to Jim's excited outburst. "I dropped mine in my zippered pocket with my tobacco and my lighter. No one else was near it. Father, the hand of God is here! Is it not?" His eyes were focused on the priest. He crossed himself again.

The priest pulled on his heavy leather mittens and drew the fur hood over his shock of red hair. "A miracle? Perhaps. Ask your friend. He's an engineer and a scientist. Surely he can explain it to you." He nodded at Jim and disappeared into the night.

— ♦ —

Jim sat on the edge of his hard cot, wondering if he would ever be warm again. Something was stirring deep in his memory. The music from the small choir had taken him back--, back farther than he wanted to go.

He fingered the gold coin, examining it in the dancing light of the lantern. He reached for the light switch and flicked it on. Perhaps he could find the explanation in a better light. The small bulb remained cold and dark.

He thought of Nester, still sleeping off his hangover. There would be no power in the village until he struggled awake and thoroughly tested the faulty electrical system. That would be tomorrow night. He frowned at his watch. It was 11:30. Was it a.m. or p.m.? Did it really matter? Then he remembered. It was evening again.

He cursed the isolation of this tiny village. Back at the base it was easier. The nights might be endless, but at least there was a routine and an artificial luster that kept the time orderly and measured.

He dragged himself off the cot and found a bottle in his luggage. It was evening and they weren't going anywhere for a long time. He could justify a stiff drink now. It would help him pass the empty night again. He could smell the faint aroma of hot copper from the boiler of water on the old stove. Jim tried to visualize the women he would meet on the sun-drenched beaches. There was always an abundant supply of available female flesh. Most were eager for companionship and easy to bed.

He wondered how long they might be delayed in Calgary. He pictured Ingried's slim figure. She would be happy to see him when he arrived, willing to share her bed, but more eager to open the expensive gifts and accompany him to the fancy restaurants she enjoyed. Still, there was something else in the back of his mind, a faint image that seemed to be pushing these sensuous beauties away. He lay back on his pillow and closed his eyes. Angie's naked figure appeared before him, climbing into the warm bath.

He sat up, cursing his imagination, cursing the isolation that was flooding him with these amorous fantasies. He had no idea how her body might look, but he was certain it would be a poor comparison to the cultured tanned beauties to be found on the beaches. Still, Angie's pleasant smile stirred his senses and filled his mind with the memory of her perfume and soft hands.

Jim rifled through his luggage, then seized his shaving kit. He was certain nothing was going to happen between Angie and himself, but he felt the need to get cleaned up anyway! He sponged himself off in the chilled bathroom and scraped the stubble from his face with a cold razor.

When he returned to his tiny cubical, he was shivering again. The room seemed to grow cooler with each passing hour as the icy wind probed its frozen tentacles between the logs. He cursed his thoughtless companion, sleeping off his hangover in the cold cabin. The restored electrical system might move a little warm air through the primitive heating system and melt some of the frost from the wall. Nothing would change as long as Nester was asleep in his cold bunk.

Jim's trembling fingers were pouring the first drink when a shadow appeared at the door. The motion caught him off guard and his unsteady fingers splashed a trickle of liquor over the shaking glass.

Angie's warm voice caressed him from across the room "Hello, Jim. I'm going to use the bathtub. Is anybody else in there?"

Jim laughed at her question. The tub still had a layer of last summer's dust ringing the bottom. He tried to focus on her face in the dim light from the lamp. It seemed she was always smiling. He wondered if that was what made her appear so sensuous. He realized that he seldom smiled anymore.

"No. I think that old tub gets pretty lonesome." He looked at the fashionable bag in her slender hands and wondered what silky undergarments she might have carried with her into this frozen wasteland.

"Wasn't the music beautiful. I can't wait until tomorrow. The concert will seem so special on Christmas Eve. Thanks again for bringing me in to the village, Jim." She moved in and sat on his bed. Jim wondered if she knew how she was stirring his senses. She reminded him of an innocent child and he guessed her flirtations were harmless.

"Would you like a drink?" he asked, raising the bottle.

"No. Thank you." she answered. "I hardly touch liquor any more." Her words dashed Jim's hopes for an easy seduction. Liquor had always been his best accomplice with women.

For a few minutes she relaxed on the heavy blankets chattering happily, scarcely listening to his replies. She seemed more interested in conversation than an affair. Jim was relieved when she finally picked up her bag and moved away to the stove. He could have that drink now, maybe it would calm his racing mind. He heard her filling the ancient tub. He sipped his mellow rye, trying not to think of Angie discarding her clothing only a few meters away.

He tidied up the clutter in his tiny cell, certain he could smell her perfumed shampoo. He let his mind wander into the tiny bathroom and imagined the nude woman soaping herself in the warm tub. He found an extra pair of socks and wrestled them on against the chill of the night. He slumped back in the hard chair and tried to concentrate on the drink in his trembling hand.

A wave of light flooded the dim hallway as the bathroom door creaked open. In a moment Angie appeared in his doorway.

She was wearing an oversized, white terry-cloth bathrobe. Her damp hair was piled high on her head, bound up in a small towel, exposing her soft neck and delicately formed ears. She looked younger, silhouetted in the light from the hallway. He was aware that she had not bothered to knot the belt on her robe. Her arms were folded casually across her breasts, barely keeping the revealing robe closed. She looked warm and inviting, but it was her bare feet that caught Jim's gaze. She wore neither socks nor slippers. Her legs were exposed up to her shapely calves.

It seemed ridiculous. Jim was shivering under several layers of clothing while Angie appeared completely at ease, her damp body wrapped only in a light bathrobe. He studied her ankles and the graceful calves outlined in the dim light from the bathroom. He was certain he could smell her damp hair over the steamy odor of the bath. Her wrists and ankles were slimmer than he had expected. In the light from the hallway her flesh appeared sculptured in white marble, well formed and more attractive than any woman he could remember. He wondered if the rest of her body was as shapely and sensuous.

For a moment she stood smiling at him in the doorway, then her full lips parted. Her voice was relaxed and friendly. Jim's pulse began to race. Perhaps his fantasy was about to come alive.

"Jim, I wouldn't mind that drink now. Do you have an extra glass?"

Jim stammered a response and his wooden fingers fumbled for the tumbler. He poured a generous shot and extended the glass to her, hoping to brush his fingers against her warm hands.

She stepped across the room and reached for the glass. Her arms moved away from the robe and it fell open. She took the glass from Jim's hands, then moved past it slipping her soft arms around his neck.

"Jim, would you like some company tonight?" She blew the words into his ear, soft and steamy and full of sweet promise. Jim found her in his arms as the robe slipped away. She was naked beneath it.

— ♦ —

They lay quietly after their abrupt lovemaking, pressed together in the chill of the room, listening to the wind driving the endless snow against their warm enclave.

"Jim, that was wonderful. I'll never forget this night. I feel so contented. It's as if there are just the two us, floating through space in this warm bed. I feel as if we can do anything we wish. Don't you find a special magic up here in the north, especially at Christmas."

Jim did not share her love of the north and Christmas had long ago lost its magic, but he was reluctant to break the spell. She chattered on until she began to coax Jim's life story from him. She was easy to talk with. He answered her probing questions, reluctantly at first, but a soft nip at his ear or a warm hand on his flesh soon relaxed him and made the telling easier. Finally she settled quietly against him and grew still. He realized he had told her everything about himself. He felt as if he had revealed his most personal thoughts including his dreams and failures. He realized that she had told him nothing about herself.

"Angie," he challenged. "You have weaseled my whole life's history out of me and all I know about you is that you like the north and still believe in Santa Claus. Tell me about yourself. Is there a man in your life now? Was there ever one?"

She laughed into his ear again. Jim wondered if there was anything about life that Angie didn't find amusing.

"Jim, I'll tell you all about myself. And answer any question you want, but it will cost you!"

"Okay," Jim responded. "I want the whole story. Name your price."

"Jim, you have to make love to me again." She slipped her warm hands between Jim's legs.

Jim made love to her again, slowly now, knowing that she was his for the night and there was no need to rush. Slowly, because he wanted to explore all her body. He was eager to learn about every intimate detail. Eager to please this soft sensuous woman who never seemed to frown or display any negative emotions. When they had made love again, Jim drifted into an exhausted sleep.

— ♦ —

He awoke to the sound of Angie dressing at the side of his cold bed. She saw him stirring in the soft light of the lamp.

"Jim, I have to go now." She leaned over and kissed his ear. "Jim," she whispered. "I don't kiss and tell and I won't follow you home."

She seized her bag and fled, pausing at the doorway to give him a quick wave and an adoring smile.

Jim hurried to the bathroom then back under the covers. The bed seemed strangely empty without her. He realized just how attracted he was to this smiling nurse who never seemed to stop her endless happy prattle. He looked at his watch. It was 4:00 a.m. He remembered the glasses of rye he had poured earlier, for Angie and himself. He reached for his glass and sipped the fiery liquor. When he had consumed the mind numbing grog, he seized Angie's untouched drink and gulped it down. He lay back in the cold cot, pulled the heavy covers over his head and drifted into the deepest sleep he had experienced in months.

♦ ♦ ♦

## CHAPTER EIGHT

Jim struggled awake, reluctantly abandoning the sensuous dreams that had enraptured his night. Somewhere in the distant fog, a familiar insistent tapping pulled him back to consciousness. His bleary eyes tried to focus on the ice-covered beard that had appeared in the doorway.

"Hey! You still sleeping? The sun will be up in a few weeks," Nester chuckled at his own twisted humor. "Get dressed! We got an invitation to dinner. Geezer says they are roasting half a fucking moose."

"What the hell time is it, Nester?" Jim grumbled. "You got to be the only guy I know who would want to eat a moose this early in the morning." There was no reply, only the sound of Nester clattering through the cupboard, searching for coffee.

Jim's shaking hands found the pack of matches on the small table. His clock told him it was 11:20 and he assumed it was close to noon. Time had become meaningless in this land of perpetual darkness. He piled on more layers of warm clothing and plodded out to Nester and the welcome pot of scalding coffee. When the caffeine had jolted his system awake, he stumbled across the frozen village, trying to keep pace with Nester's racing steps.

The feast of wild game was uneventful. He watched silently as Nester attacked the mountainous roast, wolfing down great chunks of the rich meat as if he had not eaten in weeks. His hosts were not great conversationalists and seemed satisfied with Jim's occasional nod or awkward smile to the familiar parade of guests who dropped in to share a cup of steaming tea. Jim was grateful for the space they accorded him. His thoughts were was still under the chilly comforter where he had passed much of the night pressed against Angie's feverish body.

When the meal was complete, Geezer excused himself, fumbling for his tobacco. He returned and slumped by the fireplace spreading his trembling fingers to the open flame.

"Well, lads, the wind is dying down again. We should be in the air by breakfast. Let's all take in the priest's little party then grab a couple hours shut-eye. We can gear up for an early departure, seeing as you're more anxious to travel than most of my silent passengers."

Jim rose to his feet, trying not to betray his interest in the changing weather. He hurried outside. A savage gust ripped through the trees then skidded away, stirring the upper branches and moaning into the wilderness. Jim waited for the next onslaught. The blast never reappeared, only a feeble cold breath from the frozen lake. He examined the distant sky, filled with a myriad of winking stars. The moon's arrival would grant them six hours of adequate light to illuminate the faint runway. They would be airborne by 4:00 a.m., 6:00 a.m. at the latest.

His spirits were soaring. Their chartered flight to the Caribbean had left without them, but Nester had assured Jim that he could rebook another vacation with an hour's notice. He paused and allowed his gaze to sweep across the quiet village. Now there were no scheduled flights to meet and no reason to hurry. He felt a strange calmness that was more than the solitude of the evening. He remembered Angie's soft curves and the taste of her sweet breath. She would warm his bed again if he invited her. Jim walked silently back into the cabin and accepted another cup of boiling tea. He tried to avoid the sight of the small tree in the corner and the faint images of Christmas that seemed to radiate from its lush branches.

They finished their last drop of the scalding liquid and stepped into the cold of the arctic night. Nester scoffed at Jim's offer of assistance in the gen room, leaving him to wander through the village, trying to rationalize some of the events that had begun to challenge his agnostic beliefs. He returned to his tiny quarters, located the bottle of aspirins and poured a generous shot of rye into a chilled glass. He swallowed the tablets, then chased them down with the burning liquid. Despite his racing mind, he drifted into a restless sleep.

— ♦ —

He awoke hours later and fumbled for his clock. Ten minutes after six. The significance of the time slowly dawned on him. Christmas Eve...!

Jim slumped on the edge of the hard cot trying to comprehend the meaning of this special evening and to remember why it had once stirred such a myriad of emotions deep within his soul. There had always been something special about the coming of this sacred eve. Jim felt a faint remembrance of the magic the season's arrival had once bestowed upon him.

He examined the spartan room and the drab white walls. They

would not be spending the wondrous evening in the glittering casinos of the Caribbean as they had planned. The wild desire to flee this remote location had vanished. It had been replaced by a vague uneasiness, an empty feeling he was unable to define.

He walked to the washroom and splashed cold water on his face. He knew they would soon be airborne and on their way to the Caribbean. He tried to recapture the wild anticipation he had felt earlier, but the sensation had vanished. Now it seemed his soul had become one gigantic vacuum, almost devoid of feeling or passion. He brushed his teeth and dressed for the service, struggling with the emotions that were again stirring in his soul.

Jim examined his pale reflection in the faded mirror. His face looked sadder now. His eyes told him he was no longer a young man. He touched his greying temples. Where had the years gone?

He turned away from the mirthless image and retreated to his room. He tossed the last of his clothing into the gaping suitcase. He could be packed and ready to leave in a matter of minutes.

The desire to flee had returned. Thank God they would be gone in a few hours. He was certain that the tiny village could not hold any more surprises for him, but he would soon discover how terribly wrong he could be. The darker spirits of Christmases past had not yet dealt with Jim Thorndyke....

— ♦ —

Jim abandoned his silent room and drifted into the noisy chaos of the church. The setting was reminiscent of Christmas scenes everywhere. Small children were careening around the slippery floor while the older ones gathered in excited knots waiting for the service to start. Laughing parents called to the milling throng and tried to restore order, but they too were much in awe of the season and the special night. Their shouts were wasted and only added to the noisy confusion of the evening.

Young women were carrying steaming kettles of tea from the kitchen and lavishly distributing it upon the congregation. Everyone had a cup in their hand and Jim accepted his from a smiling girl with luxurious dark braids and beaded moccasins. She wished Jim a Merry Christmas and then quickly turned away, apparently overcome with her own boldness.

Jim tasted his mug of the bitter brew. He thought again of their missed flight. The Christmas parties would be in full swing in the Caribbean. Everyone in the glittering casinos would have a drink in their hand too. The desire to flee this village of strangers was returning.

The magnificent tree beckoned to him over the squeals of the noisy children. It was a splendid sight, despite cold dead electric lights whose only radiance was the dim reflections from the glow of dancing candles. The coating of glistening tinsel pirouetted in the warming air and gave the magnificent pine a shimmering spirit of its own. He stood awkwardly to one side, trying to merge into the shadows, his embarrassment growing as more people began to acknowledge his presence. Small children peeped around their mother's skirts staring at this stranger who had dropped from the night sky to spend Christmas with them. Jim remembered the adoration in Little Fawn's eyes. He wondered how many of these babes also had the mistaken belief that he was a Christmas angel.

He fixed his gaze on the main entrance, praying for Nester or Geezer to arrive and share his uncomfortable dilemma. His patience was soon rewarded in an unexpected way. Angie swept happily into the small cathedral. She was still dressed in her drab parka and bulky sweaters, but she looked radiant. She searched the packed church until she found Jim then excused herself from her host. In a minute she was before him, taking his hands in her own and gazing up at him with her familiar happy smile.

Jim felt the butterflies returning. He remembered the crush he had carried for Lois Jackson in junior high. Each time she had approached, his knees had turned to rubber. He removed one of his hands from Angie's warm grasp and steadied himself against the rough log wall.

Angie's face was flushed, glowing with a warmth that radiated across the room. He wondered if he had helped put the color in her cheeks or if the spirit of Christmas was the sole explanation for her dazzling features.

"Oh, Jim, I'm so looking forward to this service. Won't it be one of the most beautiful things we have ever witnessed."

Her voice was stilled as a murmur swept across the packed church. Two of the elders marched in, each carrying a magnificent rack of flickering candles. They set the glittering display at opposite sides of the podium and began to organize the milling congregation, urging everyone to their chairs and benches.

Angie hurried Jim into a seat, closer to the front of the packed church than he wanted to be. She smiled and waved towards the door. Jim turned and gaped as a princely stranger marched across the room dressed in the full regalia of a Scottish Piper. There was something vaguely familiar about the proud step of the newcomer; then he realized who it was. Geezer MacLeod….

Somewhere in the old man's battered luggage he had located the complete attire of a Scottish Highlander. The kilt, matching cap and short socks set him apart from his companions in drab buckskin. His costume was complete, even to the glowing brooche and dazzling white sporran he wore proudly at his waist. The dour old Scotsman seemed transformed. The stained whiskers were washed and combed into a neatly trimmed white beard that contrasted against his dark plaid. He stepped proudly, even arrogantly into the congregation. The Tartan had changed him into a picturesque and romantic figure. He marched straight as an arrow, taller by inches than when Jim had first seen him. This was a MacLeod of Harris and Skye! Here marched a proud western clan member descended from Vikings; elegant in his kilt of red and yellow lines on a green-blue-black ground. Jim watched his haughty movements and he could almost hear the skirl of bagpipes wailing across the frozen lake. He looked at Angie's appreciative smile, then turned away scarcely able to believe the transformation.

When they were seated, an expectant hush fell over the congregation. For a minute there was complete silence, then Jim detected a flickering movement from the back rooms. A small procession of wavering candles danced out of the darkened hallway. The tiny parade appeared, leading Father Stait to the pulpit. The stately priest had a natural dignity that had always impressed Jim, but he was not prepared for the charismatic spell the man cast over his congregation. Father Bob was adorned in radiant white robes and his powerful shoulders towered over the tiny attendants with their flickering candles. He strolled to the pulpit, placed his massive hands on the maple frame and gazed out over the assembly.

The priest greeted the crowd in English and then in Dene. Jim fell under the spell of his hypnotic voice and wondered if the Catholic Church was aware of who they had sent to this remote land. For a moment he was overcome with regret for the man's missed opportunities. It seemed such a waste, banishing someone with his potential to this wilderness. The thought was fleeting. Perhaps this was where God intended him to be.

Jim caught himself just in time. He could not allow his mind to think in such dogmatic terms.

He began to examine the crowd around him, perhaps this action would calm the rush of memories the service invoked. He glanced to his left. Two of the largest Dene Jim had ever seen were settling into the protesting bench. They were dressed in fine beaded buckskin and fancy moccasins. Jim estimated that each of these men must weigh well over one hundred and fifty kilos, glowing and fit, looking like professional wrestlers who had just dropped in on their way to the ring. Their faces were filled with wonderment, completely engrossed in the priest's opening remarks. The priest had switched to English. The massive pair exchanged glances and nodded sagely.

Angie squeezed Jim's hand, eagerly pushing forward to the edge of her seat. The familiar happy smile had again set her face aglow. Jim could smell her rich perfume over the cool air of the church.

The priest's words cut though his thoughts. "*And the glory of the Lord shone around them.*" Jim watched the rapt pair of giants nodding in agreement.

He began to wonder where he had lost the exhilaration of Christmas that was so evident in this small church and in the faces of the congregation.

"*Fear not, he said, for born unto you this day in Bethlehem.*"

Jim tried to remember when a Christmas service had really meant something to him. He recalled the years when he had tried desperately to recapture the feeling with each approaching Yuletide. But it was like trying to grip a handful of powdery sand. The harder he squeezed, the more it seemed to flow through his fingers, until finally he let it go, dusting off the last remembrance with a flick of his cold fingers.

The memory of his last Christmas with Anne and the kids came surging back to him....

Anne had taken the girls ahead to his parent's farm. He had driven across the prairies from Calgary to meet them. It was Christmas Eve. The cab of his truck had been crammed with presents and the radio flooded the night with carols. He was looking forward to a long vacation; time off in the comfortable home of his parents. Twilight had fallen early. By the time he reached Regina the fading sun had vanished into a bank of fog and soft snowflakes. The farmyards drifted past, glowing red and green pools that silhouetted the barns and farmhouses. Each field of winking light seemed to be trying to outshine the other. The winding road took him close to some of the homes. He passed so near that he could look inside, where he imagined small children dancing past the sparkling trees.

Just briefly, during that peaceful journey, the spirits of Christmas had embraced him for a time. The wonderment was there again, before the whiskey and his harsh words had tarnished another shining opportunity. He recognized, as he drove to that small village on the snow-covered prairies, that their marriage was shaky. Alone in the warm cab, with the soft flakes drifting past, and *Silent Night* resounding through the console, he acknowledged to himself that Anne was not the problem. He knew he was to blame. He looked down at his hands, clenching the wheel. He would try harder. For the sake of the kids at least. He would try to make it work!

He did try, but before the holidays were over he had pushed them one step closer to the divorce neither of them wanted.

"*You will find a babe wrapped in swaddling clothes and laid in a manger.*" Jim heard a sigh escape someone's lips, almost a moan. He realized that the sound had slipped from his own throat.

Angie squeezed his hand and lay her head on his shoulder while Jim fought to control his emotions.

They fell under the spell of the priest's voice, and were again enchanted by the miracle of the violin and the wondrous choir. When the performance ended and the violin quivered into silence, a spontaneous round of applause filled the church. Jim found himself applauding and blinking the tears away. He looked around the chapel trying to conceal his face and emotions from Angie.

The clapping had subsided, a hush descended over the congregation. Father Bob raised his hand, appealing for their attention.

"I'm now going to ask everyone to join us in the singing of a few carols. We will distribute the song sheets."

The priest and two of the elders began circulating through the crowd, reorganizing the tiny congregation. The priest approached Angie and Jim. He handed them the small booklets.

"Perhaps the two of you would be kind enough to separate and share these sheets with those who do not read English. Jim, would you make yourself comfortable between the Trembley brothers?" He gestured to the smiling giants in his aisle and spoke to them in Dene. Jim looked aghast. They had seemed totally absorbed in the priest's words, Dene and English.

"Jim, I'm afraid they don't understand a word of English. They are just visiting our parish for the holidays."

Jim rolled his eyes and moved down the aisle squeezing between the imposing trappers when a common gasp escaped the lips of the congregation. A flash of color pulled his eyes back to the towering tree. The lights on the great pine flickered magically and then winked out. Once, twice and then a third time. The youngsters squealed with joy, enchanted by the mystical moment.

Jim knew it was not the spirit of Christmas that was causing the winking lights on the tree. Nester had started the cranky generator and applied power to the system.

Each electrical circuit serviced several homes and every cabin had a timer set to close their individual breaker, staggering the loading on the gen set. The church was the largest single element and the first to receive electrical power from the remote generating plant. All the breakers were open, except for the one feeding the lights on the majestic tree. In a minute Nester closed the breaker permanently and the tree began to sparkle and shine in all its splendor. It was an enchanted moment and Jim felt the thrill of the small children who viewed the lighting of this tree as a Christmas miracle.

The congregation knew that the other circuits would soon be closing and the priest directed everyone into the night to watch the lights come on across the village.

Jim reluctantly shrugged on his parka and allowed Angie to pull him into the crisp air. The chapel was located on a small rise, higher than the rest of the village. The crowd pressed to the side of the church, eager to watch the Christmas lights brighten the sprawling wintry scene. The wind had died away; not a breath of air stirred the branches of the sparse pines. The moon had not ascended the faint horizon, but the northern lights dazzled the boundless sky. It was a familiar sight to the inhabitants of this remote village but the dancing display drew a gasp of delight from Angie's cold lips.

They waited expectantly. Then the magical event began. One by one the strings of lights flickered on across the scattered village. Every cabin was ringed with the colorful streamers adorning the house and adjacent trees. Each new section flared into view to the squeals of joy from the children and murmurs of approval from the elders. At last every light was on and the entire village transformed into a glowing pool of winking lights; a Christmas jewel in the barren northland.

Two weary figures came trudging up from the gen room. It was Nester and his assistant. The remaining helpers had been left behind to monitor the gen set. The crowd recognized their achievement and broke into another ripple of applause.

Nester strutted over to Angie and Jim. There was a touch of arrogance in his weary stride. Two little girls in his path crossed themselves and curtseyed. Nester pretended not to notice, but he was beaming. He was used to completing complex projects for the company and had received his share of accolades, but this was the first time he had been accorded the status of an angel. Jim could see he was relishing the moment. Nester chuckled self-consciously and shook Jim's hand, wishing him a Merry Christmas. He smiled at Angie.

"Nester, you did a wonderful job fixing the electrical system. Everyone in the village thinks you are a miracle worker," Angie gushed.

"Oh! Really!" he chuckled "Well! Merry Christmas!" He did not waste time on false modesty. He was quite willing to accept their accolades.

The crowd was filtering back into the church. Father Stait took the opportunity to hand Nester a carol sheet and place him in the congregation.

The caroling began. Jim found himself crushed between the giant trappers. The powerful frontiersmen seemed eager to raise their voices in honour of the evening and the smiling encouragement of Father Stait. Their beefy forms pressed against Jim and he was aware of the overpowering odor of raw buckskin, so potent that it watered his eyes and closed his throat. The good priest seemed to delight in Jim's dilemma. His amused smile went beyond the bounds of rapture in the joy of the music.

The lengthy service drew to a reluctant close. The hot tea reappeared from the glowing stove in the back room. Angie led Jim into the cool night and he sucked in the welcome fresh air. They snuggled together, her warm hand squeezed into his mitten. The pressure of her silken fingers brought an added magic to this special evening.

Jim looked across the lake, examining the battered plane hunched expectantly in the snow. It didn't seem so cold now with Angie standing next to him. Her face was serene and the smile had been replaced with a look of rapture. Jim was aware of a grandeur in the wild landscape that he had never sensed before.

He examined Angie's radiant features and studied her gentle expression in the light of the remote stars. He realized then that she was beautiful! It was a sensual beauty that flowed from her soul and radiated over her lovely face. The northern lights were dancing again, their flickering patterns casting faint shadows on the snow and sending a strange unfamiliar chill up his spine. They rolled across the sky, a shimmering pattern that seemed to herald the coming of Christmas on this most sacred of evenings.

Jim examined his watch in the pale twinkle of the stars. It was past 10:30 p.m. In a few hours it would be Christmas day. He tried to focus his weary eyes on Angie. He realized this was the first time he had ever stood in the arctic night with anyone and truly appreciated the splendor of the North.

The ghostly wind had vanished without a trace. The northern lights shimmered across the endless stretch of black ice where the distant glow called his attention to their magical ballet. Legends told that on nights such as this, one could hear the distant lights ringing like miniature bells. It was an easy myth to accept and tonight his spirit was open to the fables of the north and the beauty of this special evening. In his imagination he could hear the bells, tinkling over the distant horizon.

He snapped back to reality. The chimes were not in his imagination! The faint sound of Christmas bells tinkled from the sky. This was impossible! Surely his mind was playing tricks on him. Thank God he would be in the Caribbean in a few days.

He listened again. The sound had vanished. Jim breathed a sigh of relief and examined the plane waiting on the ice. He shuffled uneasily on the crisp snow. The sound returned. It was the sound of bells! A rhythmic tinkling, like sleigh-bells in the snow or the background sounds of a kindergarten Santa Claus play. They seemed so real. He looked at Angie. A look of wonderment was playing across her features. She turned to him, squeezing his hand deep inside the warm mitten. A small gasp passed over her sensuous lips.

Where was the sound coming from? He almost expected to see Santa Claus gliding across the sky. He watched Angie's astonished face as she strained to see past the lights of the scattered village. Then he saw the mystical presence--.

It appeared as a smoky shadow, a mysterious vapor that seemed to tremble over one of the distant cabins. The image was only visible for a second before it flickered away and melted onto the rooftop of the next cabin.

The shadow seemed to be flitting from rooftop to rooftop. It couldn't be! He closed his eyes and reopened them quickly. The faint form was still there, moving across the dark sky, like some ghostly specter without dimension or substance. The sound of bells followed the specter across the rooftops. He felt Angie's hand press into his own. She was staring at the village, watching the same ghostly spirit gliding across the tree line. The sound of sleigh bells reached their ears again, like some distant echo from the stars. They exchanged astounded glances. Their voices were locked in their throats. When they looked again, the shadow seemed to melt away, fading into the dark pines. The sound of the bells dissipated.

"Jim?" she whispered, her voice was trembling. She seemed incapable of forming a complete sentence.

Jim didn't answer. He strained to locate the sound of the fading bells. Then the magical sound reappeared. The sound of *bells across the ice*....

They turned back to the lake. He could hear them clearly now, growing stronger and as pure as silver chimes over the frozen surface. From somewhere far, far away came the sound of approaching sleigh bells.

He stood in the silence holding Angie's hand, trying to convince himself that he was not imagining the sound. One of the massive church doors gaped open, throwing a pale silver flush onto glistening snow. Father Stait stepped into the night and stretched his stiff arms to the sky. Jim felt like kneeling before him. The priest was looking across the frozen lake. He had heard the sound too.

"What is it?" Jim gasped. He was staring at the priest wondering if he was about to witness a miracle.

"The teams!" Father Bob said simply. "The teams are coming in. We are blessed tonight. We have heard *the bells across the ice*."

The church began to empty as the congregation moved out to join them, listening for the magical sound. Slowly, ever so slowly the ringing tones grew. Then he could see them, small dots appearing in the distance. The approaching dogs began to bark, knowing they would soon be home with their comrades and comfortable kennels.

The silence about them was shattered. The bells drowned out by the laughter of the women and the happy sound of families waiting for their men and their Christmas gifts.

For a few minutes there was pandemonium as the teams pulled in. Some of the goods were hastily unloaded and passed amongst the happy throng. Soon all the laughing children had candies. Jim watched as one of the men pulled a pair of long, red flannel underwear from a sleigh. He rushed at his victim, holding them up against the embarrassed owner who had had the misfortune to place his order with the town's practical joker. The villagers roared with delight until finally the recipient seized the undergarments and crammed them under his parka. Jim watched this display of merriment, but he noted that many of the parcels were held back, then spirited away to be placed under the expectant Christmas trees.

The crowd began to disperse. Jim was left alone with Angie and the mysterious beauty of the night. The priest approached them and called out to Jim.

"Little Fawn wants to say good night and thank you and Nester for everything, particularly for bringing her grandmother in. She has already expressed her gratitude to Geezer."

Nester and Jim walked self-consciously towards the hushed church, awkward and embarrassed by the little girl's gesture. Little Fawn was with her mother. Jim looked down at the child clutching her mother's coat. Her face was radiant from the excitement of Christmas Eve and the arrival of the gift-laden teams. He knew Little Fawn's mother would not see her man coming in, but she had her daughter and her mother had joined them for one more Christmas. The tight look he had found in her eyes earlier had melted away during the priest's service. Tomorrow would still be a good Christmas for her and her family.

The little girl smiled up at them. Jim was aware of Nester standing at his side.

"You are going away soon aren't you? You won't remain in our village to celebrate Christmas day." There was a tear in her tender voice.

"No, we can't stay any longer, Little Fawn. We have to fly out while the weather holds," Jim mumbled.

Nester was watching the child closely. The hard look had melted from his flinty eyes.

"I have a present for you," she laughed. "I have a present for both of you. I helped my mother cut the rabbit fur," she announced proudly. "That is the most important part." Nester looked over at Jim. His eyes were brimming.

Her mother handed Little Fawn two pairs of heavy moose hide mitts, fringed with beads and lined with rabbit fur. The tiny hands passed a pair to Nester. The graying beard trembled a little as he thanked her. His voice had grown tight, his words unsteady.

The light spilling from the open door of the church illuminated the ice crystals forming over Nester's head. His breath seemed to be crystallizing in the motionless air. She turned and handed Jim a pair.

"Thank you. Thank you very much, Little Fawn. This is a very beautiful gift. I'll think of you every time I wear them. I'll never forget who gave me these."

The tiny face glowed with his remarks. "You're welcome," she said. She crossed herself and curtsied deeply.

"Little Fawn!" he chastised. "Didn't I ask you not to curtsey to me?"

"My Grandmother told me again, that you always curtsey when you speak to angels." She was emphatic now. Her tiny voice was filled with confidence. Her wise old grandmother had come home for Christmas and reinforced her protocol with angels.

Her mother turned to lead her away. Little Fawn was tugging against her parent's firm hand. Her mother paused in the doorway to exchange greetings with one of the villagers. The little girl peeked around, watching Nester and Jim trying on their new mitts. She flashed her radiant smile at the pair standing in the pale light radiating from the church, shrouded under the glow of the floating ice crystals. She was staring at her visitors as if witnessing a vision. Her wondrous dark eyes grew wider and the perfectly formed lips gaped open. Jim tried to guess what had caused the look of wonderment in the little girl's eyes.

Then he heard the strange resonance. It was the sound of an electrical arc spitting across a small gap, mingled with the tinkling of tiny bells, a bottle of champagne being opened on New Years Eve. The foreign sound was a puzzling mixture of beautiful tones, but none he could identify. He looked over at Nester. The strange buzzing sound seemed to be emanating from somewhere in the cloud of ice crystals forming over Nester's cold shoulders. Jim squinted in disbelieve. Just above Nester's shaggy head, amid the floating ice crystals and frost, he was certain the small silver cloud was crystallizing, turning into a perfectly formed glowing halo. He watched the ring of shining white light form into a precise circle over Nester's rugged features.

Jim glanced at Little Fawn. Her face was beaming in the doorway. Her own convictions had been verified. Nester was staring at Jim. A twisted grin showed through the heavy beard. Jim started to reach up. Surely he didn't have a halo as well!

The second door opened, sending a flood of light across the steps. Nester's halo vanished! Nester shook his head and glanced at Jim, blinking his eyes as if to reassure himself that they were still functioning. Jim could tell from the expression on Nester's face that his own halo had vanished. He looked at little Fawn. She waved a tiny hand and granted them one last farewell smile.

"Hey! Come on. I'll pour you a real Christmas drink!" Nester's voice was tight and unsteady.

"Come on Angie. Come and have a drink with us. It's Christmas Eve now!" he encouraged.

"No. Thank you!" she laughed. "Haven't you heard. Mary Sunchild has gone into labor. I have to see how she is doing. Wouldn't it be a miracle if she had a child on Christmas Eve!" She flashed her familiar smile at them and hurried into the crisp night.

"Hey! Too bad," Nester laughed. "She ain't a bad looking chick for this part of the country."

Father Stait appeared in the doorway. The lanky frame seemed to fill the entire structure. He moved down the steps and strolled over the drifts towards them. The night had grown quiet again. They could hear the crunch of his boots on the crisp snow.

"Red Bear has something for you, Jim. I believe it came in on a sleigh. He has asked that you drop over and see him."

Jim frowned at the priest. He knew there was no point in asking why. He had been commanded to visit him. He looked to the northern lights. They were fading again. The electric flickering had died away. He mumbled an excuse to Nester, turned and plodded across the pine-sheltered walk to old Red Bear's cabin.

A faint yellow light fell from the cabin window, leaving a golden trace on the pristine snow, like a scarf discarded by some mystical fairy. He stepped to the cabin entrance, took an uneasy breath and rapped on the solid pine door.

♦ ♦ ♦

## CHAPTER NINE

The heavy pine door glided open, silently inviting him inside. Jim squinted into the dimly lit chamber. He could see the old man seated in a comfortable maple rocking chair near the fireplace. The weathered lips curled into a warm smile as if he had been expecting Jim. The medicine man's face was lined with wrinkles, cured to a bronzed leather by campfire smoke and northern winds. Jim guessed his silent host was into his eighties. Despite his advancing years and weathered appearance, he still sported a full head of white hair and the lean body seemed to radiate an energy found in men many years his junior. Heavy braids trailed down his back. A few strands of black were threaded into the silver cables, dark reminders of his youth, when he had known a very different way of life. The rich braids fell over a faded buckskin jacket and he wore matching leather britches almost white with age. A new set of hi-topped moccasins graced his feet, heavily beaded and trimmed with white rabbit fur.

He focused his piercing dark eyes on Jim. They sparkled with a wisdom accumulated from countless generations who had walked the circle of life before him. There was a genuine warmth in his features that immediately put Jim at ease. Jim examined the old man's smile and perfect teeth; white and glinting like the polar ice caps, making the weathered face appear even darker in the pale light of the lamp and the flickering radiance from the fireplace. Jim stepped inside and closed the heavy door behind him.

Jim squinted into the crackling fire then nodded to the buckskin clad figure. He was eager to receive whatever small gift the old medicine man might have for him, so he could finish packing and flee the web the village seemed to be spinning around him.

The thin hands motioned to a comfortable chair by the dancing fire, but his host remained silent. Jim settled into the cushions and robe that draped the cozy seat. There was something about the feel of the old chair and the atmosphere in the neat cabin that put him at ease. The two men were separated by a roughhewn coffee table with several books displayed on the dark pine surface. Two of the volumes were hard cover, the others paper backs. None of them appeared to have been read. Jim suspected that the old Dene was illiterate. He recognized recent copies of National Geographic and MacLean's on the same table. These were current issues and he guessed that they had just arrived on the sleds from Fort Simpson. A small stack of lined scribblers and two fat pens were crowded into a corner of the same table. Perhaps the old man intended them as gifts for children in the village.

"Merry Christmas," Jim greeted the smiling figure. He unbuttoned his bulky parka. It was warm by the fire, but he had not yet overcome the chill of the frigid night.

"It's a beautiful night out there. I really enjoyed the service." He was certain the old Dene did not understand English, but he felt like a fool sitting there, saying nothing.

"Hummph!" the old man responded pleasantly, as if in total agreement with all of Jim's opening comments.

Jim relaxed in the welcoming chair and examined the cozy cabin. The door to the bedroom Nester had occupied was closed. He wondered where the giant husky had gone. The rough log walls of the cabin were covered with the trappings of a passing civilization; hand-made snowshoes, rusting traps, lanterns, furs and axes. A small Christmas tree was set up in the opposite corner. Someone had decorated the tiny pine with silver ornaments. The decorations were slowly revolving in the gentle air and reflecting the red and blue flames dancing in the fireplace. There were no signs of running water or electrical outlets.

He looked down at the old man's side. A faded buckskin knapsack spilled its contents on the floor next to his moccasins, revealing two fresh packages of tobacco, a few magazines and several gifts the old man had not bothered to unwrap.

Jim settled back on the soft cushions. Silence reclaimed the room, the hush broken only by the snapping birch logs on the fire. The old man reached a lean hand down to the pouch at his side. He dipped in and removed several objects, including a bulky piece of mail. The slender fingers carefully replaced the contents in the bag then extended the letter to Jim.

Jim's hands trembled as he drew the packet closer, flipping it over to read the address in the flickering light from the fireplace. He had already guessed what the envelope represented, even before he recognized Tania's hurried handwriting.

His fingers began to shake. She had not abandoned him! He was so moved that he could feel the tears welling up and he had to blink them away in order to read the hasty penmanship on the front of the envelope.

It took a full minute for his shaken mind to realize that he was holding his most precious Christmas gift. The envelope was deliciously plump and adorned with a heavy frill of postage. He stared at the letter, running his fingers across the bulging envelope, fearful that it might all be an illusion. His heart was pounding. A missing portion of his life was coming together again, multiplying the joy of the season a hundred fold.

It was Tania's letter! He tore it open with trembling fingers. There were at least ten double-sided typewritten pages squeezed inside. He folded the papers back and crammed the precious sheets into the taut sheath. He pushed the envelope securely into a deep pocket of his parka. He would devour it page by page, later, in the privacy of his own room. Now it was enough just to know that it had finally arrived.

He was so overcome with emotion, that the absurdity of the letter's arrival escaped him. Then the slow realization spun from the depths of his fogged brain. He withdrew the letter and examined the small packet again to be certain that it was real.

"The teams brought this in? How could they? How could they know I was here? How did they even get it? That's impossible!"

The old man had been browsing through the rawhide bag on his knee, mentally cataloging the items and removing those that caught his interest. He slowly raised his head in response to Jim's rude statement. A faint puzzled look crossed his brow as he tried to comprehend the reason for Jim's agitation.

"Hummph," he responded. It was a noncommittal monotone. An acknowledgment of Jim's question, but no indication that he understood his deep concern.

"This letter is post marked December 23. That's yesterday! The postal service couldn't get it out of town that quick. They can't do anything on time." Jim remembered the slow pace of the mail crawling through the arctic. "That was just yesterday!" He shook the envelope at the old man who seemed unmoved by his outburst.

Jim slumped back in the chair again. He felt a flush of anger at Tania. She always left everything until the last possible moment. She never seemed in a hurry about anything no matter how important it was to everyone else. Probably out partying with her friends while he waited, desperately impatient for this most cherished gift. His precious letter had only been dropped into the mail yesterday. He shook the package at the old medicine man seated in his comfortable rocker.

"This was postmarked yesterday. The teams were in the middle of the wilderness. They couldn't possibly have gotten the letter. It was just mailed from Calgary, yesterday!" he snapped.

"Hummph!" the old man stated once more. It seemed an acknowledgment that perhaps Jim had a point, but not a major one. The letter was, after all, resting in his hands.

Jim looked at the placid face and heavy braids. Maybe Zary was involved in this outrageous conspiracy. He knew he was wasting his time shouting at the illiterate old Dene. There had to be a logical explanation. He would sort it out when he called Tania in Calgary.

The ancient figure rose stiffly to his feet and removed a huge pipe from the mantle on the fireplace. Jim watched as the lean fingers began blending one of the new packets of rich tobacco with his own mixture of dried leafy green material. Jim could smell the deep cloying aroma of the moist tobacco. The fresh packets had come in on the sleds. He was certain the old man must have welcomed the arrival of the new pouches judging by his own withered supply.

He watched the practiced hands packing the bowl. When the gaunt fingers had completed the task, he raised the pipe for Jim's inspection, perhaps to take his mind off the letter that seemed to be causing him such anxiety. The pipe had a long stem, nearly the length of his forearm. It was magnificent, carved of polished cherry-wood and decorated with tiny designs engraved into the gleaming surface. A massive eagle feather hung from the center. It was an elaborate looking calumet. Jim wondered who had found the time and skills to carve it so beautifully.

The old man smiled and thrust the pipe towards Jim. "Smoke?" he inquired pleasantly.

Jim didn't smoke, but he was reluctant to refuse the generosity shining in the old man's eyes. There was something cozy about this snug cabin. He could visualize himself living out his own retirement in such an agreeable environment. He was no longer in a rush to get back to the cold cell in the priest's manse. His tiny room seemed to bring a flood of unwanted memories each time he dozed on the hard cot. Jim nodded in affirmation. He would share a pipe with his silent host.

The mystery of the letter whirled around him again, leaving his senses spinning. He struggled for the answer. Maybe the postmark was wrong. Perhaps Nester had gotten it in his mail by mistake and left it for him in the cabin. Nothing made any sense. He remembered the mystical presence circling over the village. Maybe, just maybe. He dismissed the idea!

A match flickered in the darkened room, snapping his attention back to the pipe and his aged host. Thin lips sucked on the heavy mouthpiece and coaxed the bowl into a smoldering glow. The old man dragged deeply upon the cherry-wood stem and then presented the ornate pipe to Jim. It was more than just passing the elaborate pipe. It was an offering accompanied by a smile and a slight bow. The lean fingers bestowed the great calumet upon him as if he were a fraternal brother.

Jim accepted the pipe in what he considered a respectful manner. He sucked the great cherry stem. It tasted like tobacco, tobacco mixed with some grassy weed or willow bark. Perhaps the old man was reluctant to use up all the scarce, expensive tobacco at once. He was extending his supply by adding his own natural blend.

Jim had never smoked. The habit disgusted him, but he sucked in a mouthful and held it a brief moment before exhaling. He was not used to the smoke in his lungs. He grew lightheaded and dizzy. A faint tingling pulsed though his extremities. He felt as if he had stood too quickly after a hot bath or had held his breath too long. It was a strange feeling, but not an unpleasant one. He passed the pipe back to the practiced hands and watched as a slow smile crept over the wrinkled features.

Jim looked around the room again. His eyes had grown accustomed to the faint light. He examined the animal skins on the walls. He knew what they were now! Not decorations, but trophies of the old man's skills, like the silver hardware and ribbons he kept in his own showcase, when he still had a home. He could sense the medicine man's comfort amidst his mementos, his crackling fireplace and the complete solitude of the North just outside the solid log walls.

Red Bear was about to draw his second puff from the mystical pipe. Jim watched him with interest. The old man seemed to be demonstrating the correct way to smoke the great pipe. He looked over the bowl at Jim. There was a touch of arrogance on his weathered face. He elevated his chin, placed both lean hands on the pipe and sucked until the bowl glowed. His eyes never left Jim's. There seemed a challenge in his every motion. He held the smoke in his lungs for half a minute and finally exhaled the rich mixture. He extended the pipe to Jim again in a formal fashion.

Jim accepted the challenge. "What the hell," he mumbled, "so far this has been a completely whacko trip. I may as well get hooked on nicotine as well."

He received the pipe slowly with both hands and raised it towards the old man. He was rewarded with an appreciative smile followed by a slow nod. The ancient Dene seemed to be enjoying Jim's company. Jim carefully placed the stem in his own lips, jutted his chin arrogantly at the weathered face and sucked in a long puff. He held the raw smoke in his lungs until his head began to swim, then he exhaled again.

"Top that, Ancient One," he gasped.

The elderly medicine man smiled into Jim's eyes. Jim felt completely at ease in the old man's presence. He was no longer a stranger with a foreign tongue. He had become a fellow traveler, moving across the mysteries of the universe with him on Christmas Eve. He looked through the cloud of smoke he had blown towards the buckskin clad figure. It had not dissipated like the first puff. It seemed to be hanging before him like a friendly mist. He stared into the vapor. The light must be playing tricks on him! The unfamiliar kick of the tobacco had left him light headed! He was certain he could see the reflection of a magnificent Christmas tree developing in the curling smoke.

The shimmering tree looked vaguely familiar. It was draped in angel hair and the lights were bubbling in a familiar, but almost forgotten manner. The image grew clearer within the thin cloud. Then he recognized it. It was his grandmother's tree, back on the old family farm. He had not thought about it in years. He had not seen such a magnificent pine since he was a child. His grandmother always had the world's greatest tree, taller than most and loaded with gleaming decorations acquired over her lifetime.

As the smoke dissipated Jim swam reluctantly back to reality. He watched the old medicine man puffing on the pipe again. He was smiling at Jim through the vaporizing smoke. This time Jim reached eagerly for the pipe; there was something in that powerful bowl that made him feel good, helped him clarify his thoughts. A couple more puffs and he would be ready to wrestle with the ghosts of Christmases past.

"You know tonight is Christmas Eve," Jim stated. "Down south everyone will be rushing through the malls buying last minute gifts they can't afford, using credit cards they shouldn't have." He knew the old man didn't understand a word he was saying, but it no longer mattered.

"Hummp!" the old man responded. He rose slowly to his feet and tossed another log on the fire. The dry birch sent a shower of crackling sparks spiraling up the chimney. The red shower seemed a picturesque invitation for Jim to remain in the cozy cabin.

"You know it's really great talking with you, Old Man. Did you know Christmas has become one of the most stressful times in our lives. There are more suicides than any other time of the year and a lot of marriages break up over the holidays. That's when my own started to come apart," he laughed bitterly. "One New Years day, after I had been partying all night."

"Hummph," the old man answered before placing the pipe to his own lips.

"I used to believe in Santa Claus too," he continued. "Yeah, I was probably the last kid on our block to give up on the old cuss. You know where I work now? I work right next to where he is supposed to be. Way up there, north, way north of here even, near the North Pole." He jabbed his hand to the north wall and the watery eyes watched Jim's animated motion with interest.

"That's where he should be, too. Living in one of the most remote peaceful places in the world and keeping his own mystical council. But you know, I have never once seen him up there. No one has. Not one of us has ever found a trace of him. Can you guess where I last saw him?" He waited for the old man to respond, but he seemed totally absorbed in the sweet pipe.

"I found him in Toronto. Yeah, bloody, foggy old Toronto. In the friggin great zoo they call an airport. The old twit looked pissed. His vanilla breath would a melted the paint off a Sherman tank. He was hawking some high priced pieces of junk from the Orient. It was pissin down rain, like it always does out there every Christmas." The old man seemed to be studying him again.

"Not much wonder Christmas has gone to hell. I used to think it was me screwed up the season, but it's as much his fault as mine you know!"

"Hummp!" the old man responded and passed him the pipe again. He leaned over and slowly picked up one of the scribblers and a fat pen. He appeared to be jotting down a few notes, recording Jim's comments. Jim knew this was impossible, for the old Dene seemed ignorant of the English language.

Jim wondered what kind of notations the illiterate old fingers might be inscribing in the text, but he was too eager to secure the pipe again. He took a long puff, held it in his lungs and then exhaled, watching expectantly to see if he could create the crystal ball effect again. It worked! The mystical cloud formed and he could see a scene within the vapor like the projected image on some imperfect background.

The setting was familiar. His old office was next door. He was back in the SunLife mall in downtown Calgary. He remembered standing in the same alcove with Anne while she listened to Christmas carols.

Now there was a towering artificial tree reaching to the top of the gleaming steel and chrome structure. Someone was playing Christmas carols on a thundering organ and the spectators were lined along the upper level. His gaze swept across the crowd. He could see the magic of the season on their faces.

He recognized a familiar figure. His tipsy senses slowed, reeling in surprise. He looked again. God! It was Anne! She was clutching her purse in her hands. A large shopping bag was languishing at her side, practically empty, but guarded as if possessing treasures of great value. She had lost a little weight. Her face no longer had its usual sunny glow. Still, the old physical attraction was there.

"Lord," he thought. "She's wearing that same old coat she wore when we were together."

It was starting to show its age too. He looked at her shoes. They were a little scuffed. She was obviously by herself, listening to the music. The carols had brought tears to her eyes. She always had been emotional at Christmas. The music stopped. Some of the crowd turned to leave and Anne moved away with them.

The organ started again, the powerful pipes swelling the melody through the building. The tune was *Little Town of Bethlehem.* It was her favorite carol. He had often heard her singing it at Christmas. Over and over to the children when they were still babes. They never seemed to grow tired of her happy voice.

Anne returned and leaned against the rail, totally engrossed in the music. She was staring, not at the organ player, but out into the snow falling in the bustling Calgary street. Her mind seemed far away. He tried to guess what she was thinking. He wondered where she was living now and if Brandon was still with her. The thought of the great dog tugged at his heart.

He remembered their Christmases together. She wasn't really that bad a person. A little disorganized, a poor money manager, but there was nothing mean about her. He wished he could take back some of the cruel things he had said to her in the past. She hadn't even answered him, when he had hurled the insults, just turned away and sobbed as if her heart was breaking. God, she looked as if she was about to cry now. She dabbed at her cheek and he knew the tears in her eyes were droplets that he had helped place there. He felt his own eyes welling up.

She moved away, brushing her face with her dark gloves. He followed her image for a time; a TV camera panning a moving object. She was still shopping. She walked into a small specialty shop and approached a rack of leather coats. He knew how much she had loved leather things. She sorted through the rack until she found a beautiful suede jacket in her size. She held it up to her shoulders and looked into a full-length mirror. The color suited her. Her smile returned and her face brightened a little.

"God," he thought. "Buy the damned thing. Brighten yourself up a little."

She looked carefully at the price tag and quickly placed it back on the rack. Maybe she was short of cash.

Sometimes his cheques were a little late, but he had sent the last one on time. Just the faint remembrance of Christmas had made him do so. His own account was flush and he felt guilty about the small fortune he would spend in the Caribbean. He wished now that he had sent her a little extra for Christmas. She reached into her purse and fumbled out a bus pass. He would follow her home. Maybe he could see how she was doing. She pushed open the gleaming steel doors and hurried into the falling snow. He tried to follow her, but the vision would not permit it. Her departing figure gradually melted into the heavy flakes and he was left with the image of the snow-covered traffic crawling down the icy Calgary street.

Red Bear was extending the pipe again. Jim seized the long stem from the frail hands and eagerly inhaled, quickly blowing out the cloud of smoke and searching for the vision again. It reappeared. He knew he was in Anne's apartment.

The room was sparsely decorated. He recognized the old couch. Where is the money going? Then it hit him! Tania had hinted at it. Most of the alimony was passed directly to her daughters, Christine, the struggling young artist whose talents were still not well known and Tania, the determined student with two years left in college.

He swallowed hard and looked around the room again. Why hadn't he taken better care of his family and his daughters? He felt a deep sense of guilt, having passed the burden to Anne.

The little tree in the corner was hung with sparse decorations. He recognized several. There were some of the first ones his daughters had made when they were still in Brownies. The first small angel Christine had created topped the tree. A small cushion, shaped and tasseled like a Christmas tree adorned the worn coffee table. Anne had picked the colorful pillow up during a trip to Minot, one New Year's holiday long ago. It had been washed a few times. The last year they were together he had asked her to throw it out before his friends arrived. He thought it had gone into the garbage, but she had saved it. God, why is she living in the past?

Brandon was there, dozing on the couch. Jim felt another tug at his heart. God, I miss that great dog! He was still big and powerful, but he looked a little overweight. Anne couldn't give him the exercise Jim had done. He could see the white whiskers dotting his chin. How old would he be now? Nine years, ten perhaps?

He wondered if there was still time in his life to take Brandon for walks in the country once more. Time to watch him spook the saucy squirrels or stare down the bold magpies. He was certain the giant shepherd would still remember him, even after all this time. If only he could touch him once more, run his fingers though the shaggy mane....

He remembered the struggle within himself before he gave the dog up. He knew he couldn't take Brandon where he was going. The dog was better off with Anne and the kids adored him.

He looked at the faded couch again and remembered an earlier Christmas, just after they had purchased the sprawling piece of furniture. The kids had been young, still babes by comparison. He was dozing on the couch when they came to him. Two loving little Smurfs in matching pajamas. Their hearts had been filled with love and excitement at the approach of Christmas. He had opened his arms to the pair and they had clambered onto his knee, nudging one and other for the most comfortable spot on his lap. They were soft and warm, oversized puppies bursting with love. He felt completely at peace and proud that he was able to make them happy and provide them with all the things every child deserved at Christmas.

He could see the lights blinking on the familiar tree, even the one that always gave him trouble. His daughters clung to him, filling his own heart with the true meaning of the season. Anne was in the kitchen. The smell of her baking filled the air. She was singing softly. "*Little Town of Bethlehem.*"

His daughters knew that they had little time left before they allowed themselves to be tucked reluctantly in their beds. Not until the cookies were out and almost cool upon the tray. Only after they had sampled them, just to be certain they were good enough for Santa. Only then would they have to endure the torturous wait until morning. Now they were content to snuggle quietly in their father's arms, totally unaware of the bliss they were bestowing upon him.

The scene faded. Reluctantly, he stared through the dissipating cloud and into the sad eyes of the old medicine man. God, Jim thought. Perhaps he is able to read my visions as well. For a moment he was embarrassed, but he seized the pipe again, eager to see if there was not one happy illusion left to balance the depressing scenes he had just endured. Perhaps there was something positive remaining in this pipe that would offer him a brighter future. He exhaled the smoke and looked hopefully into the twisting cloud.

This time it took him a long while to recognize the scene. It was a company retirement party, with the gaudy emblems on the drab white walls and the familiar table crowded with bulky presents and poorly worded telegrams. The booze was liberal. The company had learned that without it, attendance could be sparse, embarrassingly so. Jim Loehr was seated in the spot reserved for vice presidents. He had gained a little weight and his hair was thinning. So he had stuck it out and made it to vice-president. Jim was a little surprised, he had never guessed that Loehr would do so well. But this could not hold his attention. Something about this party did not seem right.

This retirement banquet seemed different from the dozen or more he had already attended. But it was a subtle change that took him some time to discern. The awkward speeches and background were the same; then it hit him! There were no women present, no wives, daughters, sweethearts or girlfriends.

"Must be some confirmed old bachelor," Jim thought. He felt a touch of pity for the lonely old codger who would receive his cold shiny watch and then fade into an empty retirement. They were clapping loudly and raising their glasses in the time honored tradition. Jim knew it was the retiring guest's turn to speak. He watched the tipsy figure stagger up from the table of honour. The man was tall, with a course white beard and long hair that needed a trim. Despite the lean frame, he had acquired a beer gut, showing under the ill fitting business suit. He felt a tinge of embarrassment for the lonely figure, then shock.... He recognized himself, another fifteen or twenty years in the future!

He looked around the room again. Now his gaze was filled with panic. There must be some women there, surely at least Tania and Christine would attend. Certainly he and Christine would have made up by then. Tania would never abandon him, would she? Where was Ingried? After all the time and money he had spent on her. Even Anne might have come. Maybe she could have forgiven him by then. The company always paid the airfare.

He searched desperately around the room, then breathed a sigh of relief. One table was empty. It was near the head table. There were wine glasses and half eaten desserts. That was it. They were all in the washroom. That was why he was waiting to give his speech. Women had the annoying habit of disappearing into the bathroom at a time like this. They all left together, like a flock of tittering birds escaping some boring scene. Jim felt a little better.

He stared at the women's washroom and waited hopefully. The door cracked open and he smiled expectantly to himself. There were eight seats at the vacant table. He knew who would be there!

The portal boldly gaped open and his heart fell like a stone driven to the depths of despair. Irwin Quick and Gerry Caouette hurried out, zipping up their flies beneath their heavy beer guts. Gerry belched loudly and Irwin chuckled, hurrying back to his glass of premium scotch.

"No! God in Heaven!" Jim pleaded. There were no women there! Some of the men were using their washroom.

So this is how it ends! Nothing but a bunch of drunken buddies who are here as much for the booze as to wish him well.

He felt something streaming down his face and touched his own tears. Surely he must have remarried. What had happened to him? For a moment he felt anger, then a total wave of despair washed over him.

The old chief was tapping the pipe into a stone ashtray. The bowl was empty and growing cold as was Jim's heavy heart.

The tired eyes looked sadly into Jim's. He smacked his thin lips and cleared his throat. He looked as if he were about to speak. Jim waited expectantly for another "Hummph."

He rapped Jim harshly on the knee with his bony hand. "Communication!" he muttered. "You got to learn to communicate with people that mean something to you." The old man rose stiffly from his cozy seat and walked to the mantle over the fireplace. He set the pipe reverently back in its place of honour then stood with his head bowed, staring sadly into the dying coals.

Jim seized his parka and touched Tania's letter, just to be sure he had not imagined it. He decided to try the old man one last time.

"This letter! How did it get here?"

The old man gave him a blank stare and then relaxed back in the maple rocker. His command of English seemed to have failed him again.

"The letter!" he waved it frantically in the air in front of the solemn features. "How the hell did this mail get here?"

The tired eyes examined Jim's agitated features. They seemed to reflect a world of sadness. No response.

"The priest said you had something for me that came in on the sled. Did the teams bring you this?"

He was favored with the same blank stare.

"The teams. You know, the teams!" In desperation he made the sound of a barking dog "Woof! Woof! Woof!" and tried to imitate a musher cracking his whip over the racing dogs.

The old man looked at him with sad pitying eyes. He shook his head slowly, no. "Woof, woof, woof?" he repeated in disgust, then sank back into his comfortable rocking chair.

"How then. How the hell did this get here? In the name of all that you consider holy, old man, tell me how this bloody letter got here!"

For a long moment the old man seemed to be pondering his words. Then he pointed to the roof and traced a long slow arc from the chimney down to the fireplace, ending on the hearth. He placed both hands on his lean belly.

"Ho! Ho! Ho!" he muttered.

Jim turned and fled into the empty night!

♦ ♦ ♦

## CHAPTER TEN

Jim fled across the frozen landscape, driven by the hard knowledge that he had seen his future and found it empty and cold. He knew it was a prospect without hope, a future created by himself. More troubling even than the empty future was the brutal realization that he had lived for almost fifty years ignorant of life's most basic principles. He had squandered the opportunity to share in the bounty that provides sustenance for the soul itself.

His trembling hands fumbled open the church door and he stumbled numbly past the empty pews. The faint lights in the chapel reflected the perfect tranquility of the evening. The silence was absolute. He was certain he could hear the lights winking on the great tree.

An air of hushed expectation seemed to hang in the night. The last happy echoes of the evening had died away and every corner of the church had fallen into a rapt silence in anticipation of Christmas morning. Only the great tree seemed animate, glowing under the splendor of the winking lights and throwing its wondrous radiance into the darkest reaches of the deserted chapel.

One solitary luminous feature caught his attention. The image of Christ was silhouetted over the small podium where the priest had recently given the congregation his blessing. A lonely candle illuminated this likeness; its soul purpose in this universe was to shed its flickering radiance on the divine figure of The Savior. The wondrous countenance pulled Jim's unwilling footsteps across the creaking floor and held him captive in the tranquility of the tiny cathedral. He paused beneath the figure of Christ, agonizing on the cross. Jim lowered his parka hood in a simple act of reverence.

He examined the glowing sculpture with its serene face. It was the first time he had been this close to the image of The Savior since he was a small child. His spirit was overcome with a rush of emotions almost forgotten. He looked up at the silent statue and prayed for an inner peace he could not hope to find.

"They say you are a most kind and forgiving God," Jim murmured. "Yet I can't even begin to ask for your absolution. But, Lord, if you could just show me how I might make a few little amends for some of the things I've done. The hurt I've caused people who only wanted my love and understanding," he choked on the words and struggled to continue.

"I don't know what you might demand of me in return to repay you for such a divine act, but so help me, I really would try to live a better life. And if you could find it in you to give me just one more Christmas like the ones I used to have, when Christmas really meant something to me. Well, I'd try to pay you back for that, too."

Jim studied the motionless icon, looking for any sign that his message had been favorably received. The somber face seemed unmoved.

"Well, I guess if you can't, then I should understand why."

He turned and walked slowly across the room, then sank heavily into a seat before the wondrous tree. The lights were twinkling merrily and every small decoration seemed to throb and pulse in expectation of a coming event too powerful to describe. The smell of the pungent pine needles, released by the warmth that had flooded the church during the service, filled his nostrils.

He huddled in the hushed chapel, completely aware that it was Christmas Eve around the world. He wondered if there was anyone else in the entire universe who felt as lonely and distressed as himself at this most wondrous and happy time of the year.

He reached into his parka and pulled out Tania's letter. How could she leave him guessing until the last minute? He was keenly aware how much one person's small thoughtless act could so affect another human being. This realization made him conscious of the many heedless sins he had committed and how his indifference had desperately pained those he had professed to love.

He remembered Red Bear's sad eyes when Jim had suggested that the letter had come in with the teams. He shook his head in imitation of the old man.

"Ho! Ho! Ho!" he muttered. "So, Santa, you really have survived in this cynical world, you old bugger! You're alive and wonderfully apparent to all those who still know the true meaning of Christmas! How the hell did some warped son of a bitch like me wind up in a place like this on Christmas Eve?"

He remembered the image of the white haired stranger about to give his shaky retirement speech. The recollection made him choke. He pictured the gray beard and the paunch that had formed under the ill-fitting suit. He wondered where the sad old man would go when the party was finished. To what lonely apartment would he retire and how much more liquor would it take to blot out the memories of the past. He placed his head in his hands. It had never felt so heavy and uncomfortable on his shoulders. For a moment he thought he might cry, but he seemed too drained of emotion even to weep.

For a few minutes he allowed the flood of self pity to wash over him. He heard a creak on the frozen floor boards. He looked up. It was Father Stait. His stately garments had been replaced by baggy slacks, a thick red turtleneck and heavy parka. His hands where jammed deep into his warm pockets. The rugged face looked tired, sadder than Jim could have imagined.

"Hello, Jim. Having trouble getting to sleep on this most blessed evening?" he asked. His words were flat. The charismatic tone had faded from his voice and he sounded exhausted.

"Yes, Father, sleep does not appear high on my list of priorities tonight!" He took a deep breath and tried to steady his shaking hands.

"I know what you mean, Jim. I know what you mean," the powerful figure sighed.

Jim wondered what emotions the priest might feel after the congregation had left and he was alone in his empty church. He wondered if it had been easier for him back in Philadelphia.

"You look a little shaky, Jim," the priest stated. "How did you get on with Red Bear?" he slumped next to Jim and stretched his creaky frame out on one of the adjacent pews.

"Shaky doesn't really seem an adequate description, Father. I think I may have seen the ghosts of future Christmases and I can't say I found any comfort there."

"Did you share a pipe with him?" the priest asked. He voice was casual, almost bored.

Jim examined the rugged profile of the priest staring into the pine boughs. The drained figure was slumped back on the hard seat trying to relieve the ache in his back. There was no semblance of the powerful evangelist Jim had witnessed a few hours previous. Jim wished he had had the opportunity to know him better. What a great friend he would make.

"You know about the pipe?"

"I know about the pipe, Jim. Perhaps I should have warned you, but...." His words trailed away in the silence of the chapel.

"But, you thought it was time someone taught me a good hard lesson! Right?"

"Well, something like that." the priest laughed softly. "You wouldn't have believed me anyway."

"Father!" Jim asked, struggling for the words. "When did you first realize that there was something out there. Something bigger than all of us?"

The priest slowly turned his head towards him. "Jim, it must have been one hell of a pipe!"

"It was, Father. It was." Uninvited, he began to tell the priest the story. Several times he paused, expecting the priest to interject, but the man sat motionless, silently staring into the lights of the great tree with Jim, his hands jammed into his pockets. When Jim had ended the tale he turned to his silent companion.

"And the pipe, Father. What do you think? Was there a message there?"

Father Stait rose slowly to his feet and walked a few paces towards the front of the church stretching his gimpy back and stiff shoulders. Finally he turned back to Jim.

"Jim, there was a message there. No doubt about that. There was a message there for you."

"And, Father," Jim asked, needing verification of the communication he feared he had received.

"Jim," the priest stated solemnly. "We both know you got the message. You don't need anyone repeating it for you."

"Yes, after all these years. And it took an old man who barely speaks English to get through to me," Jim mused.

"Well, Jim, I'm afraid you might be wrong on that count as well. Professor Edwards taught literature at Cambridge. Those books on his table are all written by him. He still has one or two new ones published each year!"

Jim sat silently for a minute, trying to assimilate what the priest had told him. The night seemed filled with surprises beyond his comprehension. He fell back on his standard escape mechanism.

"Father, can I offer you a night cap?"

"No, Jim, not tonight. I still have a few rounds to make. Christmas Eve. Remember!" He rose stiffly to his feet, but seemed reluctant to leave. He remained with Jim, staring into the great pine as if mesmerized by this symbol of Christmas and all the tree stood for.

"Father, did you ever know anyone who could define the true spirit of Christmas?"

"Jim," the priest answered slowly "Mankind has searched for centuries, trying to define the true meaning of this special season. Every year there are a few more interpretations," he added. "But Christmas is not definable anymore than peace or love or true happiness. It lives in the hearts of good people and small children and means something different to each of us. To some it means renewed friendship and perhaps to others religion. To many it's just a wonderful mystical feeling that they can't describe. I don't have the answer for you, Jim. We each have to look into our own hearts to find its true meaning!"

"You said it couldn't be defined, Father!"

"Yes, Jim, I believe I did!"

"Father, I think you came pretty close."

The priest extended his hand. "Jim, I have to go now. Merry Christmas! I'll see you all before you take off in the morning."

"Do you want me to wake you, Father?"

"Someone will wake me, Jim."

"Someone?" Jim quizzed, looking up to the rafters of the church.

"Yes, Jim. Someone. Someone called Old Bull. Geezer MacLeod is sharing his cabin. Now why don't you try and get some rest!"

Jim watched the departing figure, then called after him.

"Father. If I leave a couple of small gifts with you, will you make certain that they are dropped off?"

The priest stopped and turned back. He gave Jim a puzzled look but he remained silent.

"It's a doll, a doll and a watch. They are for Little Fawn and her mother. They were meant to be gifts for someone else, but...." He did not feel the need to finish the sentence.

The priest waited in the church while Jim retrieved the gifts. He whistled at the extravagant presents.

"The doll is for Little Fawn. And the watch; it's for someone who has been really good and never asks for anything for herself," Jim mumbled, trying to remember the small child's exact words.

"They will be under their tree by morning, Jim. I'll make sure they know where the gifts came from."

"No, Father. Just let it be from Santa."

"Good night, Jim. Merry Christmas!" he turned and walked towards the door. He paused in the doorway then looked back again. "Jim," he called.

"Yes, Father."

"Remember what I said about Scrooge!" The figure vanished into the night.

Jim was reluctant to abandon the splendor of the quiet church. He sat by the tree again and withdrew Tania's letter from his jacket....

Two hours later he folded the pages back into the envelope.

He retreated to the tiny room. The small electric lamp was shining on the dresser. The room was warm now and the small fan drove a constant stream of tepid air into the spartan accommodations. It was the first time the small apartment had not been bitterly cold. Somehow it did not feel right. Jim seized the handle on the heating vent and closed it tightly. He flicked off the light and crawled under the lonely covers.

— ♦ —

Nester's piping voice barked from the shadows.

"Heh! How can you sleep in at a time like this? First leg of our flight to Tahiti leaves in forty minutes."

Jim struggled up in his bed and frowned at his clock. It was 5:00 a.m. The room was as cold as ever. He knew that outside the church; the mercury in the old thermometer would be crouched in the stem like a frozen serpent waiting impatiently for spring. The cold glare of the distant moon would be pushing long shadows across the ice and snow on the silent lake.

"Tahiti?" Jim mumbled. "How the hell did you arrange Tahiti?"

"Heh! Called Lee Eady on the short wave. He was just coming back from another Christmas party. He called his travel agent. Got him out a bed and had him do all the booking from his computer. Lee and Bobbi Jo were in Tahiti last year. He said it was great. We leave on Boxing Day at 1:30 p.m. Direct flight from Calgary. Be on the beach in time to watch the moon come up. Airfare and hotel included. Even most of the meals. Just a few bucks for booze and the price is almost the same as our other package!"

"We gotta stop and buy Lee a drink in Calgary," he added. Nester stood there waiting for Jim's confirmation.

"All paid for?" Jim asked.

"Sure. They had our credit card numbers on file. Tahiti! They say it's fantastic and our rooms are right on the beach," Nester chuckled. "Come on, let's get the hell out of this berg!"

Jim struggled into his parka and grabbed his luggage. Nester was already out the door. Jim paused inside the tranquil church. The small candle beneath the image of Christ was burning low, the failing wax ornament weeping wisps of dark smoke in the motionless air. Jim found another candle on the table and reverently replaced the smoldering stub. He looked up at the massive tree. The lights were gamely winking their endless merriment into the furthest reaches of the church. The sweet sound of carols was piping in over the short wave. He pulled up his hood and stepped out the door.

Nester was tossing his expensive leather luggage on the toboggan and snapping instructions to the young man lashing it into place.

"Come on, Jim. Come on Tahiti!" Nester chuckled.

Jim tossed his bags on the sled and eager hands secured it with the others. He could see the old Norseman sputtering a trail of blue smoke into the motionless air. A small knot of enthusiastic well wishers was gathered around the shuddering plane. Jim looked anxiously through the crowd, certain Angie would be there. The pale moon threw a ghostly light over the group. Jim searched the milling throng, but Angie's soft form was not among them.

Geezer cut the engine as the sled approached. He climbed stiffly out of the cabin and wrestled the cargo door open. The windshield wiper mitts were already swiping at the watery nose.

"You lads got everything?" Geezer muttered as the helpers tossed the luggage into the battered craft. The villagers stood back while Geezer slammed the protesting cargo door and secured the handle with a piece of rusted wire.

"Well," Geezer muttered, "guess we may as well get airborne." He began to shake hands all around and squinted back to the church. A rangy figure was hurrying across the ice.

Father Stait loomed out of the shadows and handed Geezer his battered thermos. "Don't thank me. I'll just put it on your tab. Have a good flight!"

"Hey, Father, did you put some whisky in it?" Nester demanded.

"No, Nester, but I made it myself. Remember, my coffee is guaranteed to keep you awake!"

"Hey!" Nester announced. "I still got a bottle left. Let me leave it with you."

Nester started to climb into the back of the craft to his luggage.

"'Nester!" Father Stait halted him. "No! No more liquor. I've had my share. But why don't you all drop in next year about this time. I'll have a drink with you and we can finish the discussion we started before you passed out!"

"Hey! I never passed out!" Nester bristled. "I never passed out in my life!"

"Come back anyway, Nester. Come back anyway."

Nester's smile returned. "Hey, Geezer. We'll be back next Christmas. Eh?"

Geezer shrugged and struggled up the frosty ramp.

Father Stait reached into his pocket. "Jim, a short note for you. Angie asked me to say good bye to everyone." He passed the note to Jim.

Jim shook his hand and climbed into the back seat. He wrestled the seat belt on and unfolded the brief letter. In the background he could hear the cranky engine stutter up to speed.

"*Dear Jim: Sorry I couldn't be there to say good bye. Mary finally delivered a healthy son. Guess what they are naming him. Jesus James-Nester Sunchild. Be sure and tell Nester! Thanks for the wonderful time. I really think you should call your wife and your oldest daughter. Really I do! If it doesn't work.... Look me up in Winnipeg. My phone number is below. Good bye and Merry Christmas!*"

Jim folded the note and squeezed it into his pocket beside Tania's letter. He tried to picture Christine and Anne through the tears that filled his eyes.

"Nester. Mary Sunchild had a son last night," he shouted.

Nester gave Jim a blank look.

"Nester. They named him after you!"

Nester tried to hide his pleasure, but he was beaming. "Really!" he chuckled. "Hey, ain't that something."

Geezer was rummaging thought the litter on the floor again. Jim started to refuse the coffee, but the aroma was tempting. He accepted the battered cup Geezer thrust at him.

"Nester," Jim shouted over the roar of the stuttering engine. "I'm not going south with you."

Nester frowned across the dim cabin. He didn't seem surprised.

"I'm sorry, Nester. I've been doing a lot of thinking. I've got to make some changes in my life. The trip south is no longer in my plans."

"What the hell are you going to do?"

"Nester, I'm going to call a couple of girls I used to know. They both thought a lot of me at one time. Maybe with it being Christmas, they will give me one last chance."

Nester sipped his coffee then turned away. "Hey, you been talking to that damned priest way too much." Jim could see the disappointment in his friend's face.

"Nester. I'm giving you my ticket. Take someone else. You got a list of names a mile long in Calgary. Must be a couple of them that would jump at the chance." He passed the packet to Nester.

Nester brightened at the prospect. "You're giving me your ticket?"

"Nester, there's my old ticket. When you exchange them, put her name on it."

Nester chuckled. "Hey! I bet I know someone who will go with me!"

Jim felt better.

"Geezer!" Nester shouted. "You ever been south?"

"Hell, yeah! I went south three years ago just after Christmas. Didn't care a damn for it. Couldn't wait to get back up here!"

A shadow of disappointment crossed Nester's face. "Where did you go?" Nester seemed surprised that the reclusive old Scotsman had ventured so far from his familiar environment.

"Regina!" the scowling pilot snorted. "Spent a week drinking there one January. All they talked about was curling and football. Most of the women could out drink you." He spat the words out.

"Place was so damned cold everyone had their polar bears plugged in just to get them started in the morning. Soon as I was sober 'nough to remember where I'd left the plane, I headed back north again!"

Nester burst into laughter.

"No. Hell! I mean really south, with sand and topless babes and all kinds of hi proof rum served in pineapples. Grass skirts! You know what I mean."

"Oh, that's too rich for my purse."

"I got a ticket right here with your name on it. Room and meals included. Drinks are on me. You're coming! The girls will love your accent. It'll do you good!"

Geezer accepted Jim's ticket. His rheumy eyes examined the heavy packet a long moment then he slowly shook his head.

"Aw geez, Mother Mary, what the hell!" he growled. "Who'd watch your Ukrainian butt iffen I didn't go along with you? Maybe some Caribbean sun shine would help my rheumatism a little." His trembling hand jammed against the throttle and the old engine roared to life. The battered plane seemed eager to be on its way.

The droning craft carved a long slow arc over the black ice of the lake, leaving a thin trail of motionless smoke in its wake. Geezer banked once and made a diving pass over the village, wobbling the unsteady wings to the small figures waving on the ice. He applied full throttle. The plane surged around and headed into the night with the cold North Star fixed over Geezer's shoulder.

Jim sipped his scalding coffee and stared numbly into the cockpit. He realized it was Christmas morning….

Nester was shouting over the roar of the engine. Jim could barely distinguish the words, but he was certain he heard Nester shout "rum" and "grass skirts."

They would keep one and other amused till they made it south to Yellowknife. He closed his eyes and pretended to doze on the hard seat.

His racing thoughts would not let him sleep, but perhaps the solitude of the flight would allow him to organize the images that were racing through his confused mind. He needed the time to compose his words.

It would be the most important phone call of his life and he was determined not to waste it. Maybe the bells he had heard across the ice would bring him the luck he needed....

♦ ♦ ♦

*the end*

ISBN 1412008719